A CHRISTMAS GIFT

TO THE AMERICAN HOME AND THE YOUTH OF AMERICA

N. P. GRAVENGAARD

CHRISTMAS THOUGHTS

1. The Christmas Angel's: Dost thou remember?
I   WAS sitting in my study. Darkness was gathering, and it was Christmas Eve. Then it was as though a kind and soothing voice whispered into my ear: Dost thou remember Christmas Eve at home?

Do I? — Indeed, I remember it as it were but yesterday. I remember so plainly how we, all finely dressed, gathered at the long table. There father was sitting at one end reading aloud from the old hymn book while we all listened, our hands folded.

At the other end of the table grandmother was sitting, and I next to her, for I was "Grandma's boy." The old brass spectacles were sitting astride the very tip of her nose so that I could not quite grasp whether she peered through them or merely glanced above them.

When father had finished reading, grandmother spoke up — she wanted us to sing now this Christmas carol, now that; she had sung on Christmas Eve for so many, many years that she could lead us in singing them. Her voice — well, it was old, for she was past eighty, but if you say it wasn't fine, then you surely are no good as a judge of grandmother's voice.

Mother — do I remember her? Indeed, I never forget her. Gentle and quiet she sat at the table, slightly pale, her cheeks somewhat haggard. Her mother-eye wandered from one to the other, resting on each of us with a wealth of love. It was a strange look that came from those eyes surrounded by dark edges — it was so filled with love and wistfulness.

Then came that Christmas when her chair stood vacant. O, yes, I remember her so plainly. It was quite near Christmas when she closed her eyes, and her last words to us were: *"Follow Jesus!"*

Yes, I remember it all, but — O, wait just a little — it was only that — if tonight you visit those dear ones at home, tell them then that I remember it all. And tell them that we also—despite the struggle for money and the increasing lack of veneration for ancient Christian festivals—tell them that we also celebrate Christmas both in our home and in the church.

Thus I sent my Christmas greetings carried on the wings of the angel.

2. ROOM FOR JESUS
(Luc. 2, 7)

"There was no room in the inn."

No, neither was there room in the golden regal halls in Jerusalem nor in the palace of the high priest. Therefore the angels — those heavenly messengers — came to neither the inn nor Jerusalem. It is not with the angels as with the invader's hordes in Belgium — they do not intrude upon foreign soil, sword in hand. They are the messengers of peace, and visit only those who have room for Jesus.

And here we behold first of all the shepherds on the field near Bethlehem. In their hearts there was *room* for Jesus; the sweet music from Heaven above found the *way open* to these men.

They had been sitting out there watching how old and young flocked to the City of David to register on the tax list. It must have been a sore trial for them to think how God's people had come under a foreign yoke: Wasn't, then, all hope dead? Were not the living conditions of Israel so desperate; the people themselves so harassed that it must needs be impossible for God to fulfill His promises from the ancient days of yore? They bent their heads, sighing heavily.

But the sigh soared upward.

Thus they sat in the stillness of the night, bent under the sufferings of the age, as in former days Israel sat at the rivers of Babylon: Nobody dared play the harp! Nay — who would really be able to let the harp chords burst out in a song of joy — under *such conditions*? That would have been almost levity.

But the sigh had ascended up high, and the Angel stood before them saying: I can! I can make the harp play a song of joy. I come from the mansions of Heaven with a cheering message: "Fear not, for behold, I bring you good tidings of great joy, which shall be to all people. For unto you is born this day, in the City of David, a Saviour, which is Christ the Lord — — "

And then the first of all jubilant Christmas hymns was borne upon the pure lips of angels and carried all over the earth. That was the sweet *music from Heaven* which shall never die.

It shall sound for all those who sit in misery, or who sigh because of their poverty—for those who think that their life has become so turned upside down that nothing can ever be righted again—for those who sigh: No, under such circumstances we cannot sing the cheery songs. To all these it shall be said: *It is not impossible, at all!* It doesn't matter so much how your living conditions are, difficult or easy, dark or bright, nor how disrupted your life may be. What does matter, is whether or not you have room for Jesus.

You say: Alas—if He only would, but——

Remember, my dear, that at one time He was satisfied with a *manger* and with a *cross*. While on the cross He said to a miserable malefactor: "To-day shalt thou be with me in Paradise." And on another occasion He said to a woman taken in adultery: "Neither do I condemn thee: go, and sin no more!"

Fear not!

That was the first tone in the music from Heaven, and it was meant for *you*, also. Indeed, He will abide with you, too, when you will give Him room in your heart. Also you He will save into His heavenly realm. But, then tell me: Isn't there, even considering your wants and circumstances, every reason why you should sing a Christmas hymn with joy in your heart?

It was not levity that made the angels sing jubilantly that Christmas Eve: *They had beheld that which had been prepared for mankind through the love of God our Father*. Therefore, they could sing the jubilant songs.

So, try then to look beyond all the *despair* down here. Try to raise your eyes to the bright Heavens—to that which has been prepared for you through the love of God our Father. If it does happen, nevertheless, that once in a while you bend your head *downward*, then let the sigh soar *upward* — for it may thus happen that angels will visit you.

Therefore it shall be proclaimed loudly by the church of Jesus Christ — from the city on the mountain throughout all the lands of the earth — to all those who have room for Jesus: *Fear not! It is never so dark in your life that there is no room for the joyful songs of Christmas!*

3. WELL-SPRINGS OF JOY

Well-springs of joy!

It does sound a bit strange that *a babe on the knee of a virgin* might be the well-spring of joy. Ordinarily, it is a well-spring of worry and tears when a virgin sits with her babe on her knee — worry and tears for herself and for those who are related to her. But here we behold a virgin who herself has sung the joyful hymn of praise because she had been found deserving of such grace.

Well-springs of joy it was to Mary and to the aged Elizabeth from the very beginning — and now the Christmas Angel announces that it is "for all the people."

But, someone may say to us: Yes, we know that the *shepherds* were happy and that joy reigned in the *inn*, and we also realize that you speak of Christmas joy, etc., but when you say that this story about the Child in the Manger is a well-spring of joy — then, really, you go a little bit too far, and such exaggerations hurt your own cause. It isn't sensible to make it out quite as strong as that. Behold that highly praised Child Jesus nailed to the cross as a condemned criminal, His mother standing at the foot of the cross — and then tell us: Isn't it true that this Child, like so many, many others, made joy change into sorrow? Wouldn't any mother's heart break when she had to witness her son die the death of a condemned criminal? Even though no sin was found in Him, then you must admit that in this position he was a well of sorrow and weeping rather than of joy.

We answer: We know very well that His mother and His disciples mourned and wept — they could not do otherwise in that hour. But the *well-spring* of this sorrow and weeping was not in the crucified Christ. Even in this hour He is the well-spring of joy, for then He nailed our debt of sin to the cross. Then He redeemed us from the power of sin and death and the devil. It was for our sake that He allowed Himself to be nailed fast onto the cross. It was thus magnificently revealed here that the Child praised while sitting on the virgin's knee, had proved to be our faithful friend in life and death, when He became a man. Therefore, He is, also, in this the darkest hour of His earthly life, a well-spring of joy, and if we are to weep when we gather about the Christmas Child as the Crucified One in the church of the Lord — then it shall be out of the joy of our hearts.

The Christmas Child is the only one, born of woman, of whom it can be said that He has been a well-spring of joy. And that He has been throughout the life of mankind — from that very moment when in the Garden of Eden He was spoken of as the conqueror of the serpent. But He is also the only one who

"makes all earth feel joyful."

4. TO JOIN IN THE SONG

"The angels join the singing."

Well, it is easy enough for them to sing when we give the tone, for it is never too high for them. It is different when we are to join when they lead the singing. Sometimes it is a little bit hard for us children of dust—but we must learn it.

They sang that Christmas Eve: "Glory to God in the highest, and on earth peace, good will toward men!"

The first part of it is easy for you to sing, for "the glory of Christmas is God's above the highest sky." That's quite simple.

But when the angels then sing: "On earth peace, good will toward men!" you stop short; you cannot sing that. The tone is too high for you. When you look at your own life, it seems to be burdened much more with strife and worry and trouble than lightened by peace. And what do the heavenly hosts mean when they sing about good will toward yourself—O, well, it isn't much!

Then if you look beyond the narrow confines of your own life and behold the church of the Lord, where peace should be far more firmly rooted, then—what then? "The eye sees strife and only strife," and the people *speak* about peace and tremble in the thunder of cannon. They *bleed* and *scream pitifully* on the battlefield because of their wounds—and at home under the pressure of military budgets.

No, you cannot join in the singing!

But how, then, could the angels sing as they did that Christmas night? Was not the world filled with war and disturbances in those days, too? Was not the world full of souls in quest of lost peace? Yes, even so! And the angels saw it. But *they saw something more.*

Amidst all the restlessness of a disturbed world they saw a little Child on His mother's knee. In this child's eyes the sacred peace of

Heaven was reflected. So that was at least one human soul in all the millions of mankind where perfect peace reigned on earth.

Toward this, the only one, the angels looked.

When, then, you seek peace on earth, look not in the direction of the world, of the struggling masses, but look toward Jesus—not as He was that night on His mother's knee in the inn near Bethlehem—for He is there no more, but as He is in His church, in His word, and in His institutions. His church on earth is that mother's knee upon which you shall find Him, and where you, in a world filled with war and strife, shall find peace and repose for your own soul.

The angels made no attempt whatever to penetrate into the strife of the world or to unravel its troubles. Neither shall you so do. On the other hand, they tried to look into the eye of the Saviour, and there they beheld Peace—a heavenly Peace which they had not seen on earth since that evening hour when Adam and Eve were driven out of the Garden of Eden, and when one of their own kind was placed on guard with a flaming sword at the portals of Paradise. Then night fell upon earth. But Christmas Eve the new day began to arise from out of the darkness. Then they saw again a human being in the depth of whose soul reigned the Peace of Heaven, and therefore they bore their good will.

The peace and the good will, then, was in this one man, and through Him born into the millions of mankind. The angels had seen this one, and therefore they could sing as they did.

Perhaps you say: Well, I can understand plainly enough why God the Father and the holy angels should bear Him good will. But were I to join in the singing, I must needs be convinced that the Father would also bear me good will. That is what I need to be convinced about. But here I stand telling myself: The best acts in my life, the purest thoughts in my soul, are darkened by sin. What then?

Yes, that is true.

But, then, tell me: Have you not at times felt the nearness of Jesus? Was not He your soul's refuge in the darkness? Was not He like a luminous star in your life? Was He not yours — conceived within you in the sacred moment of baptism, born into the world with pangs within your soul — perhaps in the darkness of night? But then the Father in Heaven does bear you good will. He does not look at the darkness of sin within you — that, He knows, will be vanquished by the light of His son, but He looks at His only begotten Son who is the luminous star of your life — the only one, but splendid and bright.

Then you own in Him the Peace of Heaven and the good will of God our Father — and then you can *join in the singing*.

5. THE JOY OF UNDERSTANDING
(John 1, 1-14)

Who among us does not remember Christmas at home? — In my own childhood home there was no Christmas tree, but a remarkably impressive solemnity reigned above and upon all during Christmas. Sometimes I still wish that I might become a child once more and celebrate Christmas at home again, with father and mother, grandmother and all those dear ones. That cannot be done, however, for all these beloved ones are having Christmas in the mansions of Heaven — and I am no longer a child. But about these Christmas memories, I want to say: "God, let me never, never forget them!"

That was the joy without clearly conscious reasons. One was glad just because it was Christmas, but was unable to go into any further details about the reasons.

But now I am a child no more! — Are we as "grown-ups" to be satisfied with the memory of our childhood Christmas, and by witnessing the pleasure of the children — share a little of that Christmas sentiment which envelops all?

Undoubtedly, many people will answer: Yes, that is all. Christmas really is meant only for the children. Since we became experienced men and women who have become acquainted with the vexations and worries of life, we cannot thoroughly enjoy Christmas. To us, the law of life has been proclaimed in the words: "In the sweat of thy face shalt thou eat bread, till thou return unto the ground; for out of it wast thou taken."

In the hard, wearying, suffering and struggling life of the world, the unconscious joy, that is, the joy that knows of no reason, is not enough. There is a craving for a joy that knows and understands the spirit of Christmas if one is to be completely glad — that is true!

But what does the Gospel say:

"And the Word was made flesh, and dwelt among us (and we beheld His glory, the glory as of the only begotten of the Father), full of grace and truth."

That means, that the only begotten Son of God, who was with God and who was Himself God, has descended and taken up his abode among us—-not only among the children! No, indeed, also among grown-up and experienced men and women who must shoulder the burdens and heat of the day.

The Christmas message is the message that tells us that *Jesus Christ, with Heavenly power and with Heavenly love*, has taken up his abode among all working, struggling and suffering people upon earth—not like a haughty, indifferent onlooker at your work, your exertions, your struggle as we might imagine the son of the big manufacturer going into the shop looking at the toiling, perspiring workers with haughty, indifferent scorn and with a shrug of the shoulder.

No, *Jesus Christ entered the life of mankind as a benevolent and powerful participant in it*, so that you, when you look at your work and wonder whether you will be able to finish it—at your suffering and wonder whether you can keep on suffering—never shall reckon with your own strength alone, but must include Jesus therein. He has gone into your suffering, has taken up your fight and your work for the purpose of suffering, fighting and working with you and becoming your Saviour.

Therefore, He says: "Come unto me, all ye that labor and are heavy laden, and I will give you rest." That means: *All you men and women who labor and are heavy laden.*

But when I can grasp a little of this, then I enjoy Christmas—not because of the memory of vanished days, but because of the understanding of the fact that Christmas is meant just for me who have experienced how much there is *to labor for, to fight against, and to be saved from*, and how sorely I stand in need of a heavenly support of strength and love, in my daily work and in my daily struggles.

Therefore, I now say: Christmas is meant for all us grown-up men and women who take life seriously and who know what are its conditions. We cannot dispense with Christmas, at all. We offer God our praise and our gratitude for Christmas, and we do so *with the joy of understanding*.

6. THE FAITH OF A LITTLE CHILD

On the west front lay a 17-year-old boy a few days before Christmas, 1915. He had voluntarily enlisted under the flag of Great Britain, and was yearning to storm forward in the ranks of his comrades—forward to victory. And he *had* been in the front rank. Now he lay wounded and bleeding on the battlefield.

The battle was over; the stars shone, and he was thinking: Wonder, if I shall lie here and die!

Memories stormed upon him. His mother had said: "God be always with you, my lad!" and the old minister had said: "Remember there is always a window open upward!"

Upward—upward to God! Was it not as though the twinkling stars were smiling at him—calling him, as it were?

Yes, they summoned him upward.

O, how that wound pained him! Wonder if the ambulance isn't coming soon? He could hear the cries of the other wounded; perhaps that was when they were lifted up from the ground. Would no one find him? He could not stir, could not call—could only gaze at the distant stars.

Was there room for him up there? Yes, for he was sure death was approaching. "Mother," he whispered, "mother—O God—take my soul—now, just before Christmas—for the sake of Jesus Christ!"

The angels came, and they carried him to heaven. His prayer had been heard up there. His child's soul was carried upward to God.

When the famous French preacher, Adolphe Monod, was asked what had been the cause of his greatest gratitude, he said: "*I thank God that He hath given me the faith of a little child.*"

The main thing for him was not that God had given him a great task as a preacher and a theologian, but that He had given him the faith of a little child. That means: The faith that accepts the grace of God *without making objections!* —

O, thou great and rich and powerful people: Lay aside all thy bustle, all thy doubts, and all thy suspicion toward God — lay it aside, all of it, and accept the joyful tidings of Christmas with the faith of a little child — without making objections. Then thou wilt be glad.

The well known French writer, Larradan, whose pen formerly had written nothing but scorn against faith, during the war implored his people to return to the Christian faith as the only firm and saving foothold. He writes:

"I laughed at faith and thought myself cocksure. Now I no longer rejoice at my scornful laughter, for I see France bleeding and weeping. I stood at the wayside and saw the soldiers. They went out to meet death — rejoicing. I asked: What makes you so calm? And they began praying to God saying: 'We believe in God!' I counted the sacrifices of our people, and noticed that they bore them praying. Then it became clear to me that there was something comforting and sustaining in recognizing an eternal home-country, when that of the earth is glowing in the fire of hatred. This feeling is science — the science of the child.... A nation must despair if it does not believe that the torment of the earth can be exchanged for the joy of Heaven.... France was great in the days of yore. But that was a France which had faith. How about France in our own age? It is torn to pieces with want and suffering. It is a France that believes no longer. Will her future brighten? At the hand of God — only at the hand of God. — France, O, France, revert to the faith, to thy most beauteous days! To go away from God is to perish!..."

I thank God that He hath given me the faith of a little child!

THOUGHTS FOR THE NEW YEAR

1. TO SEE LIKE THE ANGELS

THE striking feature of the way in which angels see does not consist in their seeing everything, both good and evil, in this world, in a rosy hue, in heavenly glory so that they really do not see the evil as it is — but in this that they see particularly what is good and seek that by preference — let their eye dwell upon, rest thereon, with pleasure. Therefore we can sing:

To us He also smiles
With Heaven's light in His eyes.

It is otherwise with that human being who is depraved by nature. His eye seeks, with a certain predilection, whatever is wrong in his fellow-beings, dwells upon it with mischievous joy. It is an innate fault which makes it difficult for us humans to embrace one another, to smile at one another, in the manner of angels.

Suppose that we in the new year make a serious attempt to look at each other as the angels look — seeking what is good in our fellow-beings. With an earnest will we can accomplish much, especially when we are sustained by prayer.

Let us begin at home!

Perhaps it is long since you, man, have embraced your wife and given her a real *smile*. When she was your bride — in the years of youth — that was your greatest joy, but as the years went by you found this fault and that with her, and then — why, then you ceased embracing her and smiling at her. It wasn't quite as bright in your home as before. She became more and more reticent; her rippling laughter — like that of a child — was heard no more. Her cheerful songs were silent. She became rather morose and querulous. A woman cannot thrive where home is without smiles and love. You accepted the slow changes as it behooves a man of staid dignity — life teaches so much, also compromise with ideals, and the realization that the bright expectations of youth come to naught.

But, now suppose that it wasn't Life, but you *yourself* that were to blame? Suppose the change arose from the fact that you had been inconsiderate to your wife. Your eye had detected her faults and shortcomings rather than her good points? Try, man, during the new year to look at her as the angels look at us! Let your eye, diligently and willingly, seek what is good in her, dwell upon it, be jealous of it—give her all the appreciation she deserves for making the home cosy and comfortable. Try it with an earnest effort and a sincere prayer—then you will once more feel like embracing her and smiling at her as you did when she was the bride of your youth. It might happen that you would reap a *hundredfold* before the year ebbs out. It will be brighter and more snug in your house—and it will feel so good to be at home.

Or you, wife and mother, beginning to bend down and "feel old" although you are just beyond thirty. Perhaps you tell yourself: O, had I only thought then that he was as he is—but I did not know. And the children, yes—God knows, they are like him—naughty and hard to manage. Instead of staying at home to help a little with the children in the evening—he just simply skips out.— —

Hush—wait a while!

In what way did you tell him this when you asked him last to stay at home? Did you throw your arms around his neck—did you *smile* at him, saying: My dear, stay home with us tonight?

It's no use, you say—but "it's no use" is, absolutely, a term which cannot be found in the vocabulary of Christians nor in the life of Christians—nor in yours if you are a Christian woman. It helps very much to do what is good while praying—perhaps not *when you* want it, perhaps not the way you want it. But it will surely help if during the new year you look for just that in your husband which you loved when you were young—if you let your eye dwell upon it, cling firmly to it in your thoughts, carry it into your prayer—embrace him and smile at him as in the bygone days of youth.

Where love has been sown, the harvest is as dependable as is that of the wheat in the field—it is only in some cases that it proves a failure. And even though yours might seem to be just such a case where your love did not sustain him—then the love which you have sown will sustain you and your little ones—and in the course of the year your home will reap at least thirtyfold.

We always gain by sowing love—also in cases where we must needs acknowledge that our love, like the seed that fell by the wayside, bears no fruit in those upon whom it descended. But in the large majority of homes the seeds of love will fall into fertile ground, and bring forth fruit, some thirtyfold, some sixty and some a hundred.

When only we have learned how to embrace the dear ones at home and to smile as the angels smile, then we will also be able to smile at others—but first at home.

And a year in which we have tried with earnest diligence to learn the art of seeing what is good in life, to dwell upon it and to smile at our fellow-beings—as the angels smile—is a good year, rich in the grace and blessings from above.

I had just officiated at the funeral of a woman, the mother of many children, when a man said to me, "Well, now she's got a velvet-lined coffin, but while she lived she was hardly able to get a calico dress." And that was not because of poverty.

What if her husband had given her a velvet dress while she was living! Then she would have taken pleasure in it, and he would have received her gratitude. The beautiful casket she could not enjoy—and could give him no thanks for it.

But *you* don't behave like that, do you?

On another occasion I heard the widow ask one of the pall-bearers when we turned away from the grave: "How did you like that sermon?" The following day I met her son-in-law and was told that she had not liked it at all. Among other things he remarked: "She simply wanted you to put some feathers in her crown, but there wasn't any room for them." And I agreed with him.

In both instances man and wife lived together until parted by death. But love had died—happiness vanished.

Speak to each other the kindly words—scatter flowers on each other's way throughout the year, then Love groweth, and happiness in the home increases in intensity. Then you can truly sing:

Home, home, sweet, sweet home,
There's no place like home—
O, there's no place like home.

2. THE HIDDEN LIFE
(MAT. 6, 5-7)

The inscription on the tombstone erected on the grave of the great French philosopher, Descartes (died 1650), reads: *"He has lived well who was hidden well,"* or, *"He is happy whose life is hidden."*

In this lies the thought that happiness depends upon the hidden life—that this is something good which affords one a refuge.

Nowadays, the prevailing impression is that happiness is contingent upon *life in public view*; that happiness consists in the ability to attain a prominent position, in being admired, gaining wealth and winning fame. This is an absolute delusion.

Andrew Carnegie, the late multi-millionaire, said: "I have tried to make money by leading an incessantly busy life—but it did not make me happy. Now I have tried to give money away to public institutions—and still I found no happiness in that"; this is an impressive testimony from a prominent and honest man, showing that happiness has nothing to do with life in the public view.

It is this Jesus says to the Pharisees: You stake all upon *leading your life in public view*, in the synagogues and in the streets, to gain the admiration of men. For this reason you have forgotten to seek the good refuge with God, to lead a hidden life with God, full of prayer. Therefore, your public life is devoid of blessing to the people and without joy to yourselves. *You have no reward, and no happiness.*

"Enter into thy closet, and when thou hast shut thy door, pray to thy Father which is in secret." You shall seek the hidden corners of your own heart and there speak with your Father about that life which stirs in there, unseen by the world. Then you will soon realize the necessity of hiding with God the Father and of living your life with Him hidden away from the world. That is the condition for your becoming a happy man or a happy woman, and it will contribute to the bliss of that part of your life which must be lived before the public.

Therefore, this shall be my New Year's wish for you, that you *during the coming year may find the happiness which lies in the hidden life of prayer, with God.*

Many married people seem to think that their matrimonial happiness depends on swell homes and association with those more prosperous families known as "society"—"Keeping up with the Joneses." This is wrong. Attempts of that kind often lead to the utter destruction of happiness. It is true that a nice home and a pleasing circle of acquaintances are worth much, but marital happiness does not depend upon them. It springs from that life which man and wife live together unseen by the eyes of the world.

The happiest moments in the life of a wife are not those in which her husband stands upon the stage of the world, the object of praise and admiration—as the man *to whom the laurel wreath is given*; nor, in the life of the man, when his wife is considered *a celebrated grand lady*. No, the sublimest happiness in married life is due to those hours when man and wife sit cheerfully at home, hand in hand, talking about the grace of God and about their mutual love.

Many young people think that happiness and joy depend upon the number of dances they are able to attend, or upon exterior circumstances. It is not their fault that they are neither happy nor glad. It is due to the environment, living conditions, to those with whom they associate. And while all this may be of importance it is, profoundly seen, a delusion, nevertheless. It is true, also, in the case of the young man and the young woman that their happiness essentially depends upon their hidden life. If that is a life of impure thoughts, of sinful cravings—then happiness will be meagre, no matter how favorable the environment may be. There will be no calm and deep-seated joy, no real happiness. If, on the other hand, that hidden life means a life of pure thoughts and noble ambition, a life in God, then it will mean happiness even though the environment may be unfavorable.

It is a law in the life of mankind that happiness depends upon the manner in which the hidden life is lived. By creating this law, God has given rich and poor an equal chance of happiness, and has shown Himself as the friend of the poor.

King Charles IX of France once asked the Italian poet, Tasso: "Who, think you, is the happiest?"

Without a moment of hesitation, the poet answered:

"God."

"Yes, yes, very well," the king said, "but then next to God?"

"The one who resembles Him most," was the answer.

THE WORTH OF YOUR SOUL

"FOR what is a man profited, if he shall gain the whole world, and lose his own soul? Or what shall a man give in exchange for his soul?" (Mat. 16, 26.)

The first thought is that of *the infinite worth of the soul.*

In one scale of the balance Jesus places all the world with its gold and gems, its art and science, its limitless values of woods and prairie soil—and in the other, a human soul. And then He says: Behold all this splendor! Look at it all, thou yearning child of man! It is not equal to the worth of your soul.

Everything great and beautiful in life originates in the human soul. Through that, all noble thoughts and great ideas have come into being. Every work of art was formed in a human soul before it was painted upon the canvas, chiseled in marble, or written in a book. It is the stamp of the human soul that lends value to the work.

Revere that *mark of the soul* wherever you recognize it! But have reverence, above all, for the *soul* itself. That has the worth of infinity. To "lose your soul" is to suffer everlasting damage which cannot be repaired or substituted by values of the world.

The other thought is that about *exchange for your soul.*

Wherever that precious soul is demanded of you, you can give nothing else in *exchange*. There is nothing in the whole, wide world that has value enough as exchange for a human soul. Neither is there anything whose value can equal that of the mark of your soul upon your work.

If you owe your neighbor ten bushels of wheat, you may pay him back by giving him twenty bushels of corn or cash in exchange, and he will realize that he is paid in full. But this cannot be done where rests upon you the giving of your soul.

This first of all you must consider in your relation to God who gave you your soul. He will demand it from you when your earthly life has ended. If your soul then is seen to have suffered corruption, it is not fit to enter into eternal life, and you have nothing else to give God in its place. It avails you nothing that you say: "O, Lord, I know that I have been so occupied with worldly things that I have not taken care of my soul, as I should have done. But, in this way I have made $10,000 which I now donate to missionary work."—My dear, that cannot compensate for the wrong that has been inflicted upon your soul.

David understood this. Therefore he said to God: "For thou desirest not sacrifice; else would I give it: thou delightest not in burnt offering." But God delights in a prayer like this: "Have mercy upon me, O God, according to thy lovingkindness; according unto the multitude of thy tender mercies blot out my transgressions. Wash me thoroughly from mine iniquity, and cleanse me from my sin!" There is a human soul in this prayer—it is true that it is a suffering soul—but it is there.

Thus God demands that your soul be in your *prayer*, your *praise*, and your *worship*, and there is nothing else that can take its place.

The worship of the Pharisee was perfect, from the point of form. Everything was done according to rules and regulations. But it was *soulless*. Therefore, Jesus condemns it. But where He hears the prayer or sees the tears of repentant sinners, He stands still. There he stoops, and in their wailing and stammering worship He beholds a human soul that has suffered wrongs—one, perhaps, which is deeply tainted. But the soul is there, and it has worth to Him. He can heal all the wounds of the soul. And where the wounds of the soul are being healed, worship takes place. But, then, the human soul must take part.

This is true, also, in worldly things. Where your soul is demanded of you, you can give nothing else in barter for it.

You may give your wife food and shelter, dresses and footwear, but that is not enough. She has a right to your soul. Golden rings and splendid dresses cannot take its place. But if you do give her your soul — in smiling joy or in a burst of weeping — she will cling unto you with everlasting rejoicing in her heart. In this devotion she will recognize infinite worth.

Or your children! You may give them a good education, may even leave them a substantial legacy. But what God above all else demands of you, is that you give them your soul — a father's soul and a mother's soul, which they can learn to honor and to love. To give them a substantial legacy as an equivalent to this spiritual partnership is to give them stones where bread is wanted.

Remember, then, your soul's infinite worth — remember that wherever it be demanded of you, in your relations to God or men: You can give nothing in its place.

There is nothing in this world which is valuable enough to take the place of the human soul.

THAT WHICH IS HIDDEN SHALL BE REVEALED

(Mat. 10, 26)

"FOR there is nothing covered, that shall not be revealed; and hid, that shall not be known."

No one sees it, thinks the burglar when in the hours of the night he breaks into a house. It is hidden by darkness.

No one sees it, think the adulterer and the adulteress when they satisfy their sinful lust. It is hidden to others. It is their secret.

No one sees it, and no one will know about it, the young man thinks when, covered by darkness, he sneaks into the saloon.

Yes, God sees it! — Yes, God! But, to be sure, He doesn't tell the neighbors about it the next morning. No, to be sure! But, nevertheless, it will be brought forward in the light of the day — all these secrets of darkness.

If that consciousness could but be vivid and strong within us — how many criminals would then keep away from the paths of evil!

And how many secrets of darkness would be revealed to God through repentant confessions — and be *forgiven* instead of *concealed* in the innermost chambers of the heart like a guilty secret — a guilty secret only to be covered by a new transgression.

"The Lord discovereth deep things out of the darkness, and bringeth out to light the shadow of death," says Job (12, 22).

When Judas had agreed to betray Jesus, he concealed that evil secret in the innermost chamber of his heart. But Jesus saw it in there. He saw that this secret of darkness would push Judas into the darkness without — down to despair — to perdition.

Therefore Jesus made an attempt to bring out that secret from the darkness when they sat together at the Easter meal. That is my understanding of Jesus' pointing out Judas as the traitor. It is as though he would say to him: O, listen, Judas, let us bring that dark secret out into the light so that it may be forgiven! But Judas arose and went away. He wanted to keep the evil secret to himself.

Happy he or she who asks Jesus to bring forth the evil secrets from the heart so that they may be repented and forgiven—so that their power may be crushed! Then, on the great day they shall be revealed as having been *repented of* and *forgiven*—to the glory of the Lord who has released us from the fetters of the evil secrets.

But it is not only the evil secrets that are to be revealed in the light of the day. *All* secrets are to be revealed.

Does man possess other secrets than those of the darkness? Will there not be very little to bring forth in the way of good secrets from the recesses of the heart?

No, thank God, there will be thousands of them.

All those loving thoughts which you conceived in secret, and which you never found a chance to express—they shall be revealed on that great day.

All the heavy sighs and all the burning prayers which have issued forth from the depths of the heart in secret, shall be made known in the light. And they are countless. Generation after generation has witnessed parents praying for their children—O, could we but realize a small part of all that which has been fought for and prayed for in secret! Then we would be surprised to know that someone had *thought so lovingly, had prayed so fervently, and struggled so earnestly for our sake—in secret.*

All these good and pure secrets shall be revealed on the great day.

How radiantly they will testify that the human heart has not been merely the battlefield of the secrets of darkness, as some seem to believe.

And together with all the evil secrets, repented of and forgiven, they shall glorify our Lord and Saviour Jesus Christ who endowed us with the gift of *wanting to* think lovingly, pray fervently, and struggle earnestly in secret.

NOT IN WORD, NEITHER IN TONGUE

"MY little children, let us not love in word, neither in tongue, but in deed and in truth" (I. John 3, 18).

Five little girls stood in a garden telling each other how dearly each one of them loved her mother. The words became more and more emphatic until finally Bertha — the eldest of them — poking her nose upward, said decisively: "I love my mamma so much that I could die for her sake." And thus everyone was brought to silence.

But on a bench a little farther away in the garden Bertha's aunt sat sewing; she overheard it all, and then said: "It is strange that a little girl who loves her mother so much that she would be willing to die for her, does not love her enough to wash dishes for her. I heard this noon, Bertha, that you didn't want to do the dishes for your mamma!"

It is strange, indeed!

"My little children, let us not love in word, neither in tongue, but in deed and in truth."

The young man says to his bride: "I love you, darling, so much that I could carry you on my hands all through life!" — A year after the wedding it may happen that he cannot carry up a bucket of coal from the basement for her.

That's strange, too.

The young woman says to her fiancé: "I love you so much that I could die for you!" — But if it is a question of that new Easter bonnet, she cannot save a dollar out of regard for her husband's pocketbook: She doesn't love him that much.

You do not love each other enough to *sacrifice* for each other's sake — or to be a bit *patient* with each other — or to *cut down a little* your own personal demands out of regard for each other. Therefore we have so many divorces.

"My little children, let us not love in word, neither in tongue, but in deed and in truth."

Charles Dickens tells in one of his books of two sisters who are discussing how intently they wish to do something really great and good. Under the petty circumstances at home they couldn't get the chance. But if they might be sent out as missionaries among the heathens—O, how they would toil just to help those poor people! It didn't matter that perhaps they would have to suffer the pangs of hunger and persecution—if they only could show people their love.

Just then their old grandmother who was sick abed in the next room, said: "O, girls, won't one of you come and scratch my back?"

"You can do that," the one said. "No, you'd better do it," said the other. "It's always up to me—you might do it once in a while!"

That was the end of the glory—and of the love. On distant shores; under other circumstances they would do deeds of love. But in that everyday life where God had placed them, it wasn't quite as easy as all that to show their love.

We can all catch ourselves in similar shortcomings. We would like to be charitable on a grand scale if we were *elsewhere* or *differently situated*; but in everyday life—it is so prosaic just to help an old mother, or a grandfather, or some sick and poor person. And yet it is that which submits us to the crucial test.

"My little children, let us love not in word, neither in tongue, but in deed and in truth."

SEEST THOU THIS WOMAN?

(Lu. 7, 44)

SIMEON is a benevolent Pharisee, deferential toward Jesus, but icy and dignified.

The woman is a sinner, a former prostitute with whom Simeon is disgusted; yes, he sees her, all right! He knows her!

It is as when I ask someone: Do you know the ocean? and he then answers: I should say so! I have been standing in the downs watching the waves; I have seen them soaring to the height of houses while the wind whipped their foam into my eyes. Yes, I have seen the ocean — I know it, all right!

Then I answer: Pardon me, my dear — but if that is all you have seen, you do not know the ocean. You have not *seen* it while it lay calm and glittering and smooth like a mirror in the sunshine, nor have you *noticed* it when its surface was all alive with ripples, and when it roared with that hollow sound that betrays the presence of violent undertows far beneath the surface.

Thus with Simeon. That which he had seen and heard of this woman, had been brought to him, like the wind-swept foam of the sea, in the storm of evil tongues, and then he says: I should think I know her, indeed! I know to what kind she belongs. I see her — a low-down, vulgar and lewd woman!

But the undertow in the depth of her soul he had not seen; the heaving sighs from within he had not heard. He did not know how often she had been tossing restlessly upon her couch in moaning and anguish, nor how firmly she had been clutched by the wound-inflicting bonds of vice, nor how strongly she had tugged at them in order that she might set herself free.

And that was not the only thing Simeon did not see. The wind-swept foam had veiled his eye so he could not see what was really good in her at that moment despite her appearance stamped with sin. *There were bitter tears of repentance. There was warmth of heart. There was love for Jesus.*

Seest thou this woman? Seest thou this man?

How do you look at the people among whom you live? Do you notice only the uncouth exterior? Do you listen only to that which is carried to you by the wind of the evil tongues? Or do you listen to the undertow in the depths of the heart, to the heaving sighs, the hollow roaring from within?

The famous Italian sculptor, Michelangelo, once stood before a large coarsely chiseled slab of stone which he surveyed carefully, and with increasing pleasure, from all angles. "There is nothing extraordinary about this stone," a friend remarked, "what peculiarity do you notice?"

"What do I notice?" Michelangelo answered, "I see an angel within this stone, and I must release it."

It may be that our Lord Jesus did not exactly see an angel within this woman—nor does He see one in you and in me—but beneath the rough surface He saw a human soul created in the image of His Heavenly Father and after His likeness, and He said: I will release it!

By looking at the undertow in the depths of the soul and by listening to the heaving sighs from within, you will be enabled to look at your fellow-beings with ever-increasing interest and—delight!

WHAT ABOUT THE DEVIL?

WHAT about the devil?—That is an exceedingly difficult problem to the wiseacres of this world.

Recently a learned professor proclaimed from his speaker's chair that no single individual, no organization of any kind, could rid the world of the devil, but Time would—Time would most certainly get him away. And the assemblage applauded enthusiastically from out the joy of their hearts. Most likely they did not stop to think at that moment that Time would undo them long before it could ever undo the devil. That may, however, be excused, for learned people often are somewhat thoughtless—and all these were scholars.

Or was the charity of the auditors so far-seeing that it rejoiced in behalf of generations yet unborn? Well, who knows—for that kind of people also possess a heart.

Be that as it may.

But, concerning the devil—whether a devil actually exists or merely is a creature of imagination; whether he is a really dangerous foe or simply a phantom from the days of yore—I must try to make clear to myself, and you must do likewise.

It doesn't appear to be so difficult, after all, when the matter is approached without any frills and furbelows. I look at it this way: I have been baptized to renounce the devil, all his works and all his ways. That was told me at the moment of my baptism. I affirmed it in order to be incorporated into the Kingdom of God. Jesus Christ demands of me that I renounce the devil if I am to be His disciple. If, then, no devil existed, He who is Himself the Truth and the Lord of the Kingdom of Truth, at the outset must expect of me that I affirm a lie—He whose own lips never knew untruth and deceit, would ask that I in order to become a part of His Kingdom, renounce a devil who does not exist: That would not only be senseless: It is impossible! When my Lord and Saviour tells me to renounce the devil, then I do believe a devil exists, and that my own welfare now and hereafter makes it necessary that I keep away from him.

In this matter, the word of my Lord sufficeth for me!

It is my faith in this which relieves me of many of those speculative difficulties which entangle so many others. I must choose between the word of my Lord and the speculative mind of man. To me the choice offers no difficulties at all. I choose the word of my Lord—no matter whether or not the scornful laughter sounds derisively from the other side. And let me say it once more: The word of my Lord sufficeth.

When, then, I meet some of those people who claim there is no devil; that all talk about the devil is a relic of ancient superstition, I simply say: You must excuse me, but in this matter I abide by the word of the Lord. I cannot ignore His word and accept yours, and, furthermore, I have *no reason whatever* for doing so; I have never yet found that I could not depend upon His word.

And if I then consider the ways of the world, as they are—then I most certainly am not tempted to abandon the covenant of my baptism. The works of the devil are apparent to all: Murder, adultery, theft, robbery, fraud, deceit, drunkenness, etc. Many may say that these are the doings of evil people, but if we look a little closer at these evil people we will find that back of it all is one whose thralls these poor creatures are.

If I try to look into the spiritual anguish of these pitiful individuals, I am not tempted to give up my belief in the devil. To be sure, I do not behold him physically, but I see his works. To me it seems to be as when I see a building is being erected. I ask: Who is building this place? I am told: It is Mr. Smith who builds this place, and we are his laborers. I do not see Mr. Smith himself, but I notice that his work goes on, and I do not doubt that he exists. I see his laborers working, some sing and joke while others are sullen and indifferent just because it happens that they have entered into an agreement which for the time being makes them realize their obligations to Mr. Smith.

If the latter could only find a way to wriggle out of that relationship, they would feel unspeakably relieved to do so.

Thus I see the works of the devil in the life of man, and by seeing them I find no reason to doubt his existence. The evil people are his laborers. They work in order to complete his job — some singing and joking, others under compulsion. It is clear that especially the latter are the slaves of the devil. By looking into the spiritual life of these miserable ones I find confirmation of the word of my Lord that there is a devil that must needs be renounced if we are to live contentedly. It is from him our generation needs relief, and not from all that ancient gossip about him.

I said a little while ago that the word of the Lord sufficeth for me in this matter, and that is true. It does not correspond with the theories of the wiseacres, but with Life itself. From the learned infidels the cry is sounded: It isn't true. But from the depths of real human life we hear the sigh: *We are sorely troubled by the devil!*

TWO EPISODES OF THE CIVIL WAR

1. LOOTING THOSE WHO FELL

THE battle was over. Darkness expanded its misty veil over the battle-field. Victory had been won by neither army, but there were left a large number of dead and wounded.

The ambulances were sent out with help for those who fell in the fight. Where moans were heard, they went, raised the wounded limb a trifle, asked sympathetic questions and bandaged the wound as well as could be done in a hurry; then the wounded were taken to the field hospital.

But if one looked more carefully, other figures were discernible; half hidden by the darkness they sneaked about among the wounded and dead.

Who were they?

It didn't look as though they heeded the moans of the dying, nor did they raise them to carry them off to the field hospital. What were they doing, then?

They were plundering those who fell, taking from them their little articles of value: A hideous thing, truly a deed of darkness! Who would have believed that anyone could have the heart to plunder the dying.

You and I would not do such a thing. We become intensely indignant and disgusted when told of such heartlessness. "God, I thank thee, that I am not as the other men are, extortioners — — "

No, on that battlefield where the wounded lie, having been hit by shells and maimed by swords, we do not go in order to plunder and loot. That is true enough.

But — alas, there is a "but" about it.

The world is a huge battlefield. Right and left we see about us the *wounded* who are moaning and suffering from pain; they are sighing for just a little aid, a kind word, a gentle smile. They need succor — they need being taken to the hospital. They still have a remnant of the sense of honor left. There is a possibility that they may right themselves; that they may be able to qualify as good fighters in the next skirmish — perhaps to conquer where now they have suffered defeat. *But* instead of the gentle smile, the kind word, and the little aid — we took away from them whatever was left and let them lie where they were. We deprived them of the last remnant of honor, extinguished the last faint glimmer of hope. The bruised reed was broken. The smoking flax was quenched.

On Life's vast battlefield you and I may, after all, have taken part in the plundering of the wounded; or we may have gone by just like the priest and the Levite. At least we have not always done as did the Samaritan: Bound up their wounds, pouring in oil and wine, and brought them to an inn!

Old Dr. Bengel says: "I am kept constantly busy by reading proof upon myself."

Let us do likewise. Then we will be better and better enabled to heed the moans of the wounded on the vast battlefield of Life, and to bring them to the inn, to the church of the Lord where there is healing for all wounds. This is our task toward the wounded, and it was that which was in the mind of Jesus when He said:

"Go, and do thou likewise!"

2. REMOVED BECAUSE OF MISCHIEF

During the Civil War it became necessary to remove one of the officers serving under General Sherman; "Removed because of mischief" was the way it was entered upon the record.

General O. O. Howard succeeded him in command and continued to have charge of the unit until the end of the war.

Then the army arrived at Washington, where a parade was to be held followed by disbanding.

The day before the parade General Sherman said to Howard:

"The political leaders demand of me that the officer whose place you took, resume his charge tomorrow and ride at the head of his unit in the parade, and I wish you would help me out of this predicament."

"But it is my unit now, General," Howard said, "and it is but fair that I ride at its head tomorrow."

"Yes, of course," General Sherman answered, "but—are you a Christian, Howard?"

"What do you mean by that?" Howard asked astonished.

"I mean that you can bear that disappointment and let him have the honor. You are a Christian," Sherman added; "well—what do you say?"

Like a brave officer, jealous of his honor, Howard had anticipated this day with delight, but, after hesitating a moment, he said:

"Yes, looked at from that point of view, only one answer is possible: Let him ride at the head of his old unit tomorrow!"

"All right then," said Sherman, "but you will report at headquarters tomorrow morning at 9 o'clock."

The next morning at the appointed hour Howard reported that everything was arranged. The officer who had been removed because of mischief had resumed his old post.

"Very well," Sherman answered, "then you ride by my side today."

"I have no right to do that," Howard replied.

"It is an order," Sherman answered smilingly.

Thus O. O. Howard rode beside General Sherman at the head of the entire army in the parade at Washington — he who had renounced glory and right for the benefit of one who had forfeited both, so that the latter might *be honored.*

"Removed because of mischief." That might have been written upon the brow of Adam when the portals of Paradise were closed behind him. Removed from the living God because of mischief — that *was* the legend above the whole story of mankind until the fullness of time.

Removed because of mischief — from one another, from the respect of fellow-beings, from honor and enviable positions among men: That was the legend above the lives of so many — of him who had stolen money from his master's till; of him who had suffered a moral lapse, etc.

But into the life of him who has been removed from God because of mischief one came and said: It is my will that you resume your old place of the child in the arms of his Father. It is my will that you take part in the ride into the new Jerusalem. I will share my rights with you and give you my glory. Yes, thus speaks the Son of the King of Heaven in His church upon earth.

This I have done for thee, Jesus says. But then, when you go among those people who have been removed because of mischief from good positions or from the respect of their fellow-beings: How much of your glory and rights can you give to them?

You are a Christian.

We ask, almost as surprised as O. O. Howard: What do you mean by that, Lord? Too often, we ourselves think too little of it. But Jesus sayeth: Remember that you are a Christian when you associate with those who have lost the respect of their fellow-beings. As a Christian you must be able to sacrifice a little of your honor and your rights for their sake.

To be a Christian is not merely to be a child and to rest upon the arm of the Father. *It is to make real the love of the Father, in the steps of Jesus Christ, among those who have fallen by the wayside.*

You are a Christian.

Are you?

And one thing more. Howard did not lose anything by relinquishing his glory and rights like a Christian. Far from it! He gained by it. He was placed beside the supreme commander at the head of the entire army. Thus with us.

When Jesus demands of us that we as *Christians* shall bring sacrifices, then it is not for the purpose of causing us any *loss*, or to make us *advance* something for which we will not be reimbursed, but simply to enable us to receive more from Him. Such advances He changes into an income for us. We will receive a hundredfold. We will be qualified to be at the front, and by His side we approach the goal.

YOUR WORDS

(Mat. 12, 37)

"FOR by thy words thou shalt be justified, and by thy words thou shalt be condemned."

Isn't this a strange way of speaking?

If Jesus had said: "By thy works thou shalt be justified, and by thy works thou shalt be condemned", then I would have immediately conceded that this was good common sense. Actions are something tangible, something you can get the actual "feel" of, but words — why, they often are nothing but hot air.

Still Jesus says: "By thy words shalt thou be justified, and by thy words thou shalt be condemned" — so, I must accept that.

When, then, I think of the words I have spoken, at home, in the church, in the midst of the congregation, I cannot conceal *to* myself the fact that there were many empty words among them. Not only that — there were also some mean words, and when they are to be measured by Him who never sinned, and whose lips never knew deceit, then I must tell myself: There is enough right here to condemn you! And I am possessed with *fear* and worry because of my own words.

If I revert to the good words I may have spoken, it isn't much better. And still, I cannot say but that I doubtless have spoken some good words, and that they may have been of benefit to some. I am quite certain that I often have spoken good words at sick-beds, in the homes and in the church — words that were willingly listened to just because they were good words, that really did comfort those who were sick and had sorrowful souls — words that were something more than sounding brass or a tinkling cymbal — words that were inspired and filled with the warmth of my heart — words in which I myself rejoiced sincerely, and for which I could never sufficiently thank God that He gave me the grace to utter them.

But, yet—in spite of all this—it does seem to me that when my words are to be judged by Him who always spake the pure, the powerful, the pungent, and the perfect word—then mine will be found wanting. In other words: I *doubt* that those words of mine were so faultless that He who is Himself faultless, would consider me justified by my words. No, to the contrary—I must tell myself: Thou art weighed in the balance and found wanting!

Thus I find myself placed between *fear* and *doubt*—fear because of my evil words, and doubt about the faultlessness of my good words.

What shall I do, then? Shall I timidly withdraw from the words of the Lord: "By thy words thou shalt be justified, and by thy words thou shalt be condemned"?—Shall I attempt to forget them, imagine that they were not meant for me, have no bearing upon me—or shall I try to avoid them as some fearfully avoid cemeteries at the midnight hour?

No, I cannot do that!

I must have these strange words clear in my mind. I must work them through. To stand between fear and doubt, timidly withdrawing from the words of my Lord! No, that cannot be possible. Where shall I seek refuge? Where shall I seek that explanation which reconciles me with the word of the Lord, and which brings peace into my soul?

I will seek refuge in the pledge of my baptism—as so many others have done in the hour of worry and distress. I let it pass upon my lips, and the word is: "I *renounce* the devil and all his works and all his ways." But to renounce means that I break off from, separate myself from, and become a foe of, the evil one and all that is evil— also my own words. But can He, the fair judge, condemn me for that which I disavow and separate myself from, what I personally oppose?

No, it is impossible! That cannot be!

This gives me surcease. The fear of my evil words must vanish, and, thus unburdened, I go on.

"I believe in God the Father Almighty, Maker of heaven and earth.... I believe in Jesus Christ His only Son, our Lord; who was conceived by the Holy Ghost, born of the Virgin Mary; suffered under Pontius Pilate, was crucified, dead and buried; He descended into hell; the third day He arose again from the dead; He ascended into Heaven and sitteth on the right hand of God, the Father Almighty; from thence He shall come to judge the quick and the dead.... I believe in the Holy Ghost; the holy Christian church; the communion of saints; the forgiveness of sins; the resurrection of the body, and the life everlasting."

The word of the Apostles' Creed is the word of faith. And what did I say? I *believe*! It may be feebly, alas, but nevertheless—with all its frailty the heart embraces the word of faith, and doubt vanishes before this word.

Almost astonished I ask myself: Is it possible? Is it possible that I who found myself placed between fear and doubt, conquer both by the word of faith?

That word of faith has thus passed upon my lips, not like a sounding brass or a tinkling cymbal, but as a *truth of the heart*. It was not a hollow saying, it was not a faulty word, and yet it was my own. It was given to me in the early morn of my life as a gift from God in my baptism. Now it asserts itself in spite of all the evil, empty and faulty words I have spoken—reaches to the Lord Himself as an expression of the innermost life of my heart, and the answer of the Lord to this word is: By thy words shalt thou be justified!

Thus, through the words of the Lord I gained peace in my soul, and my heart bursts out its "Praised be God!"

BEHIND THE SHIELD

(Eph. 6, 16)

PAUL is imprisoned at Rome and is writing to "the saints which are at Ephesus." He beholds Christian life as one immense struggle—not against flesh and blood, that is, against the depraved elements in the life of mankind and the evil tendencies in man; no, back of flesh and blood are principalities and powers, a host of spirits trained in the wiles and the cunning of the devil, and exercising a tremendous power in the world, through evil persons.

Against these gigantic powers we must needs fight, and we must vanquish them. But we cannot do so by our own power. We must be "girt about with truth," must be clothed in "the whole armour of God." This is not an armour that can be forged from the steel within ourselves—although we say that with all due deference to bravery, shrewdness and wisdom; but in the great struggle against the powers of darkness we must be girt with something stronger. Fortified with *our own*, we sustain wounds, but win no victory. The armour of God gives victory, but protects against wounds if we know how to use it rightly.

But when Paul describes the whole armour of God, he strongly emphasizes a particular part of it, for he says: "Above all, taking the shield of faith, wherewith ye shall be able to quench all the fiery darts of the wicked." Thus it is a question of making proper use of the shield rather than of the sword. The church of the Lord has hitherto laid stress on the use of the sword, and therefore the result of the fight has often been a number of wounded souls, for the sword wounds, while the shield protects.

It is said of our heathen forefathers that they knew how to *fight* as well as how to *rest* behind the shield. They knew how to grasp all the hostile arrows in their shield while they fought; when they had fought themselves weary or spent all their arrows, while the foe still had plenty of deadly arrows to hurl against them, they knew the art of taking a rest behind their shield in the midst of the shower of arrows. Covered by the shield they gathered strength for the purpose of resuming the fight with axes and spears while the enemy uselessly wasted his supply of arrows.

I wish sincerely that we possessed somewhat more of this ability of our forefathers to use the shield, to *fight and to rest behind the shield of faith, spiritually speaking.* That would make it possible for us to give battle the thunder of which would resound in the remotest corners of the earth, as in days of yore the song and the hammer strokes of our forefathers were heard in distant countries. Then we would not use our fighting ability to plunder foreign shores, but to lead the fight against the spiritual powers of evil — to be in the front ranks during the fight that shall be fought from the sea to the ends of the earth, in which thousands must bleed because they have not learned how to use the shield of faith.

We shall make a stand against the wiles of the devil!

If I am not very much mistaken by the signs of the age, the attacks on the church of the Lord will during the present century become still more marked by diabolical cunning and cleverness than ever before. *The arrows* will be sharpened with all the shrewdness of science, directed against us with cunning, glowing with a devilish hatred against everything that is of heavenly birth, and aims at heavenly goals. Indecent jokes, cutting scorn and cleverly formulated inquiries will constitute a cloud of arrows which will darken the sun to many. They will be hurled against us through the means of literature and science, with violent haughtiness, with fierce hatred. And we — we have not that unconquerable courage which enables us to say with the hero of Thermopylae: "So much the better — then we fight in the shade!"

How shall we approach the struggle of the twentieth century?

Someone may say: We shall sharpen our arrows, make them pointed, and send them forth with shrewdness and wisdom. We shall use our common sense, meet the opponents on the battlefield of thought and cleverness, show them what is unenduring in the chimera of the atheists and what is depraved in the life without God. In the church of the Lord we have men who are not inferior to our opponents in respect to cleverness and wisdom—indeed, we have, praised be God!

But it does seem to me that many a valiant fighter will succumb in this kind of a struggle, and many plain-thinking Christians may flee, as did the Philistines in ancient days when their giant had fallen. All honor to those who defend and promote the Kingdom of God by thought, by reasoning and by wisdom! But along that way we do not accomplish much more than to humbly admit that

"Stood we alone in our own might,
Our striving would be losing."

More and more the shibboleth must be: "Above all, taking the shield of faith, wherewith ye shall be able to quench all the fiery darts of the wicked." Learn how to fight, covered by the shield! That means: All your struggle must be based upon the words of faith, all your arguments must take these as their point of departure instead of using human sagacity and the tricks of interpretation; then you will be unconquerable. And if it does happen that you become weary in the fight against the wiles of the devil, or that your arrows are all spent while the foe has plenty, then do as our fathers did: Take a rest behind the shield! Cover yourself completely with the words of faith, then no hostile dart will reach you, far less wound you. On the contrary—you rest and gather strength while the foe exhausts himself uselessly, and "all the fiery darts of the wicked are quenched."

This method of fighting is especially adapted to the people, and it is *the age of the people*, also in the church of our Lord. The future does not require a great chieftain with a host of good-for-nothings behind him, but an army whose every individual is trained in the use of the shield of faith.

When Mr. Moeller-Anderson, a Dane with a warm and faithful heart, a Dane whose quiet ways his compatriots abroad do not forget—in the summer of 1888 made regular sailing trips from Copenhagen to

Sweden for the sake of his health, it happened one day aboard the vessel that some scoffers wished to have fun with him. They may have thought that it would be an easy matter to subdue him. They, therefore, started a conversation with him, but soon their speech changed to scoffing and witty questions, daring attacks upon Christianity. Then Mr. Moeller-Anderson replied: "I don't know how that all may be, and I cannot answer you, but if you wish to know what my faith is, then I will confess my faith through the Apostles' Creed before you right here!"

The scoffers had nothing more to say!

What had Mr. Moeller-Anderson done which made them silent? Had he told them a striking joke which could not be commented upon, or had he stated a cleverly formulated truth which they could not resist? No, he rested behind the shield and the scoffers realized that *he was protected*.

You Christian man and woman from the everyday walks of life—when you meet the scoffers, then don't try to find clever thoughts with which to defend Christianity, as though that were your way to victory. In that case it would merely become a question as to which side was supported by the greatest wisdom, the most cleverly pointed shrewdness. The great struggle of the world is the *struggle of faith*, and it must by no means be changed into a chaos of personal trickery and clever stratagems. Above all, grasp the shield of faith instead of resorting to your own wisdom and cleverness. Say your creed plainly and simply, you mother of a child, you master of the home, you young man and woman among your chums, when you meet the devil and his wiles in the form of clever questions formulated so as to entangle you in self-contradictions—catch you in the net of words as formerly the Pharisees and the Herodians tried to catch Jesus asking: Is it lawful to give tribute unto Cæsar?

You often hear it said: You claim that God loveth mankind: But why, then, does *He* let some suffer in all eternity? Or, you claim that you have a good Father in Heaven who can do everything: How is it, then, that He lets His children suffer distress on earth? etc.—Say it plainly and simply: Well, I can't answer questions like these, for I do not see through all these things, but if you want to know what my faith is regarding salvation, then I will confess my creed right here before you! That's to rest behind the shield, and you will feel how blissful that is compared with the fight by wisdom and reasoning in which there is the fear of being wounded and vanquished, and of rendering harm unto Christianity by attempting an unsuccessful defence.

Behind the shield of faith: there is victory both when you fight and when you rest!

Paul was not afraid of fighting. Neither must we be. But that fight which gives victory without wounds, without one painful sensation to limit the joy of victory, must be directed from a *covered position*. And the agility necessary to enable one to seek cover behind the shield of faith is obtained only by *daily training*. Therefore, train yourself every morning to protect yourself by the words of faith before going to your work and fight your fight; and in the evening when you lie down to rest, you must train yourself so that in fight as well as during the lull, you can be covered by the shield of faith; then you will conquer the wiles of the devil, and his fiery darts will not wound you.

Thus I consider it essential for the church of the Lord in the twentieth century that it learns how to use the shield rightly whether in fight or at rest. The *struggle* of the church will then result in a greater victory and in fewer wounds than during the last century, and its *rest* will become increasingly beneficent and strengthening while its restlessness will become less nervous and less strength-consuming.

Wonder if the time has not come when the church, driven by inner friction and by enemies from without, will listen readily to the apostolic warning: "Above all, take the shield of faith, wherewith ye shall be able to quench all the fiery darts of the wicked."

I look forward to the day when the Apostles' Creed becomes the *universal slogan* for all Christian organizations. Then the church of the Lord will march forward to victory.

LOVE ME—AND TELL ME SO

AN English bishop was traveling in India to inspect the mission work, and when his journey was completed, a farewell gathering was held in his honor. On this occasion the bishop spoke on the words: "Love me—and tell me so!"

He had often asked himself whether his congregation at home really loved him. He thought it did; but sometimes he couldn't help wishing: If they only would say so! Now he wished to say, by way of a parting greeting, to the Christians: Love your ministers, and let them know that you do! They need your love, and they need to be told that you actually do love them.

This little speech reached England before the bishop arrived there. When, upon reaching home, his congregation received him with a banquet. On the wall of the hall, just opposite the main entrance door, was an inscription in large letters ornamented by leaves and flowers: "We love you, and we are saying so." That was the first thing the bishop saw, and he rejoiced.

Love me, and tell me so! That's the cry from thousands of souls yearning for love, and where the cry finds an answer the heart rejoices. Where no answer comes, life will be utterly miserable.

Once upon a time a wealthy woman met a poor orphan who looked imploringly at her. "What do you want me to give you?" she asked. "O, just like me a little bit!" the orphan answered.

O, just love me just a little bit!

I have seen that prayer where one should least expect it—I have read it in the eyes of a mother when they rested upon her grown-up daughter. She had indeed grown, was taller even than her mother. And then she had received an *education*—mother surely could be proud of such a big and fine girl who had learned so much! But a mother's heart finds no sustenance in mere pride. It required delight in the daughter—and there is delight only in love. But the girl went about so *fine* and *big* and *cold* while the mother, even as the poor orphan, implored, O, love me just a little bit!

All you nice and big children: Remember that mother and father need your love! Love them — and tell them that you do! You can tell them in a number of ways, and it will be rewarded, for in love there is a world of joy.

Love me — and tell me so! O, love me just a little bit!

I have read that prayer in the eyes of a wife: Her husband was a man in whom she surely could take delight. He was efficient; everybody admired him, women especially, and he seemed to like everybody. Indeed, she could be proud of such a husband! There were plenty of women who envied her and wished themselves in her place. And — how beautifully he could speak of domestic love — women were deeply touched, and their eyes moistened when he did so. O, if they only had such a husband — but such a one had not fallen to their lot!

He had plenty of smiles and kind words and love for everybody else — only not for his wife who sat at home. Hard-hearted, frigid and haughty he passed her by when she sat with the baby on her knee, with despair penetrating all her features, and the one prayer was flaming in her eye: O, love me just a little bit — just a little bit, O, please do!

Love me — and tell me so! O, love me just a little bit! That has been written in the eye of ever so many poor and forlorn human beings — especially among those who seemed to have become sadly superfluous in the busy life of the world. Now and then I have heard just such people say, with a strange mingling of wistfulness and joy vibrating in their voice: To think that the minister would call upon me! Nobody else ever comes here. Nobody cares about me any more!

Thus many a man or woman has been placed in that miserable kind of solitude in the midst of throbbing life. Nobody cares about me. Love me — and tell me so! O, love me just a little bit, please! That's the cry from the depth of their hearts, but it is uttered as though in some limitless desert: No answering sound is heard—there is no sign that anyone cares for them. This is heartrending.

Yes, that is true. But if these lines of mine might reach some such poor soul, then I would say: It isn't quite as bad as this. Let your yearning for love soar upward to that God who listens to the sighs of the heart of dust, and then you will hear the response: I love you—and I tell you that I do. I have told you so through my only begotten Son: "For God so loved the world, that He gave His only begotten Son, that whosoever believeth in Him should not perish, but have everlasting life."

This has been said to mankind plainly enough. And these plain words are not merely written in the leaves of the Book of Books. They are inscribed in the very life of mankind with the blood of the only begotten Son.

Such words are not merely for the happy world surrounding you. It means *you*—just exactly you who are yearning for love: For your sake these words have been spoken.

But we who are more fortunately situated—we who enjoy the love of God and of our fellow-beings, and who, in return, love those in our homes, in our circle of acquaintances and in the church—let us tell one another about it in a good and nice way. So much joy of love is lost—just because it finds no expression. For this reason so many gradually come to doubt that they really are being loved.

The congregation wrote it on the wall of the festival hall, ornamented with leaves and flowers. It went out of its way to say it in just such a way as to make its old bishop feel deeply delighted.

It pays to exert yourself in this way.

Let it be written with large letters between minister and congregation, between man and wife, between parents and children—yes, let it be written with large letters—and wind about them the leaves of the forest, the flowers of the field—everywhere:

We love you, and we tell you so! Then our lives will become rich with the joy of love.

TO BEAR BURDENS

(Gal. 6, 2)

"BEAR ye one another's burdens, and so fulfill the law of Christ," Paul says.

"No, thank you!" you say, "I have quite enough in taking care of my own burdens. If I am to be troubled with those of others in addition, life will be intolerable."

Nevertheless—do you think Paul speaks aimlessly? Or isn't it rather the case that there is something of *relief* in bearing burdens for others—something of a *gain*?

Think of a wheat field: One straw stands close beside the other. The wind-storm sweeps the field. The wheat bends down in billowy undulations under the heavy pressure of the wind, but rights itself stronger than ever before. The close-standing straws bore the pressure together. Then the wheat is harvested. A few straws are left standing. The wind again sweeps across the field, the lonely straws bend down to the soil—and lie there. They are broken. Singly, they could not resist the pressure of the storm.

Thus in the life of mankind. Great burdens can be shouldered with ease when shouldered in common while the smaller burdens may crush and destroy those who stand all alone.

There is relief in bearing burdens for others.

But you ask: Dare I, a single individual, try to shoulder the burdens in my home, in the church? Suppose that in one or more instances I were the only one to do so. The others left it all to me, although they had the same obligations that I have—what then? Will I accomplish anything but being crushed under the weight of the burdens?

How about Jesus Christ when He, *all alone*, bore the sin of mankind? He was wounded for our transgressions, He was bruised for our iniquities, as the prophet had foreseen.

But when He who was so strong, was wounded and crushed under the weight of the burdens—what will happen to me, then, when I shoulder the burdens of others? I cannot do so cheerfully and courageously and expect a satisfactory result. Rather I must flee timidly away from the burdens by recalling what happened to our Lord Jesus Christ.

Yes, if that was all that may be said about Jesus that He was "wounded and bruised" when He, out of the depths of His love, shouldered our burdens, then no doubt you are right. Then there is no prospect that you will do better.

But that isn't all.

After having been wounded and bruised under the weight of the burdens, bent to the ground, indeed, bent in death, He arose with the mark of victory upon His brow, and with *peace* and *healing* for us.

Yea, *peace and healing*!

That was the last, the ultimate result. And it is the law in His church that wherever we shoulder one another's burdens, we shall find peace and healing.

We may be wounded, indeed crushed, under the heavy pressure of those burdens. We may be bent down into the dust, but that is not the last, the ultimate result.

It is peace and healing.

Thus it is not only a *relief* to bear one another's burdens; it is the highway to peace and healing. We can extract this blessed fruit from out of the burdens. How splendid to be able to bear the burdens of everyday life with and for one another and to gain peace and healing for those who are timid and bruised. *This is the last and final result of bearing one another's burden in the name of Jesus.*

BE STEADFAST IN PRAYER!

1. *A Gain and a Protection*
O PRAY for me!

That is one of the cries that frequently come to us from the sick and the dying—sometimes because they have not themselves learned how to pray in the days that passed, but always with the consciousness that prayer is *needed.*

Pray! sayeth our Lord Jesus Christ, for it is *helpful* to pray. And on the background of nearly two thousand years of actual experience His church responds: Indeed, it is helpful to pray!

"Ask, and it shall be given you ... for everyone that asketh receiveth.... Or what man is there of you, whom if his son ask bread, will he give him a stone? Or if he ask a fish, will he give him a serpent? If ye then, being evil, know how to give good gifts unto your children, how much more shall your Father which is in heaven give good things to them that ask him?" (Mat. 7, 7, etc.)

The prayer is a *gain* to us since we have such a generous Father who will not refuse us anything good, and who has it in His power to give us all.

But the prayer also is a *protection.* "Watch and pray, that ye enter not into temptation" (Mat. 26, 41). The ability to be absorbed in prayer is a protection against temptations, and in the prayer strength and fortitude are secured with which to resist the temptations.

In complete realization of this the Apostles continuously implore us to pray.

Make the prayer a regular and constant feature of your daily life. Don't let it be a matter of chance whether you offer a prayer or not. Don't let every insignificant hindrance prevent you from saying your prayer. Many of the ancient leaders in the church of the Lord set aside several hours a day, parts of their most propitious working time, for praying—and considered that a gain. Thus Luther often devoted three or four hours a day to constant prayer. You may not accomplish anything like that, but you are able, nevertheless, to give the prayer a fixed and constant place on your schedule for every day, and then you will experience that it is a gain and a protection; for "prayer brings down from Heaven the peace of God; it brings down the strength to love and revere Him; it brings down from Above relief in the hour of distress, and it brings infinite comfort at the moment of death."

2. *What Mother Taught Me*

A chaplain at one of our insane asylums related the following:

One day when he had been preaching a sermon to these poor, insane people among whom only a few were able to make out what he said, one of them came to him and announced: "I, too, can pray!" The chaplain stopped surprised, because the man was completely an idiot. He had forgotten everything—his name, his age, his home; about these things he could give no information whatever. Somewhat doubtfully, the chaplain asked him: "What can you pray?"

The poor fellow righted himself a little and answered: "What mother taught me"; he then folded his hands and spoke the following verse with perfect ease, and without mistakes:

Lord Jesus, who dost love me,
O, spread thy wings above me,
And shield me from alarm.

Everything was forgotten. Not one event in his life was he able to recall in his memory. Everything had been left out of his soul, out of his memory—only not that one prayer his mother had taught him.

I have myself had a somewhat similar experience. It was a Dane who was not wholly demented—rather what is known in the vernacular as "crazy" — and a little more. He never did any harm, and for that reason he was sent to the poor-house instead of to an insane asylum. Whenever he found an opportunity, he made his escape, and once in a while he came to my home — once at eventide and he was then allowed to stay overnight. In the evening he sat plucking at his clothes just like a child, and he then said: "I'm clean enough, all right." A little later he said: "I ain't forgotten how to pray — want to hear me?" Then he folded his hands and spoke two little verses of the kind a mother teaches her very young child. These he could remember. It was the same thing over again: What mother taught me.

Remember this, you Christian mothers!

3. THE EVENING PRAYER: A PROTECTION

Above all, it is important to give the evening prayer a fixed and permanent place in the daily schedule of our life. When we intend to pray for something, the time at which it is done may be relatively immaterial, but if we think of the prayer as a *protection*, the evening prayer goes before anything else.

And why?

Because it requires the peaceful quiet of eventide—and the same thing is true about all kinds of silly fun and of evil. In point of time, the evening prayer meets with the tempting voices of wickedness that sound with the greatest irresistance in the darkness. A decisive battle thus takes place between the tempting voices of wickedness and the evening prayer—a battle about time; it is a Whether—Or, for to divide the time in twain in this matter is impossible. It is not possible to devote one evening hour to wickedness, and the other to prayer. Then, if the evening prayer is given a regular place in one's everyday life, it is a protection against the temptations.

Therefore the evening prayer should be a part of the child's life even 'way back in the days of the cradle. And therefore we praise the fact that the evening prayer is just that prayer which it is easiest for a mother to make a part of the everyday life of the child; this is not a mere accident, but is due to that grace of God which descends upon Christian mothers. Say the evening prayer with your child, and for your child, every evening when you tuck him or her into bed—do it even before the babbling voice of the child is able to say the words after you—and do never miss an evening!

The evening prayer which has thus been implanted in the heart of the child because of the privilege and the intense love granted to the mother-heart, and which is to be protected by that same love throughout the years to come, will prove to be a real protection to the child during its earliest youth, which is just the very time when it stands most in need of *protection* because the tempting voices of wickedness resound with the greatest power in its own breast. For that reason the time of youth is that period of our life when we stand most in need of the evening prayer.

Loving parents often are somewhat worried when they discuss the day that the children must go *out into the world*. Now and then a tear drops from the mother's eye when she thinks that her half-grown boy or girl soon must leave home. It is not because of worry for their future, economically speaking, nor always because of the thought of separation—but it is the fear; How will they come out? Will they listen to the voices of wickedness, find evil associates, forget both God and their parents so that they rather seek the *saloon and the dance hall* than the home of their childhood? Of course, you may say: It won't be as bad as that! And, praised be God—these things do not happen in a great many instances. But the danger is there, and the temptations are ever present—and many a young man and woman who during childhood were the very joy and pride of their parents, succumb to the temptations and suffer during their youth such defeat that recovery is possible only much later in life or—never:

You suffer for that through many years which only was briefest delight— —

But to comfort such parents let me say: Let the evening prayer find a fixed and permanent place in the life of the child from the very days of the cradle—then you have built a fortification about it which will guard and protect it at all times because it has become an essential part of itself. The evening prayer of its mother is the last thing the child ever forgets—that which it is most difficult to part with. It does not yield to a little push or two, but will powerfully assert its right to occupy the seat of honor in the heart, and it will insist that the quiet hours of eventide belong to it by right. And even though the child throw its mother's evening prayer overboard in order better to heed the tempting voices of wickedness, he or she will be conscious of restlessness and uneasiness in the depths of the heart, until that demand is met which the evening prayer makes. Yes, even though the child may time and again scoff haughtily at the evening prayer and thus apparently get far enough to push it away with all the silly "nerve" of the age of adolescence and to conquer it—that time will come, is sure to come, when the memory of it and the memory of mother awakens in the child's heart and revives in loving remembrance so that the evening prayer resumes its permanent place in the life of the child. The memory of mother will be a treasure to the child who only then realizes that the evening prayer proved a protection against the plentifulness of temptations. She will receive the gratitude shown her with child-like reverence, because she implanted the evening prayer in the heart of the child. That was one of the mother's deeds of love that became the greatest blessing throughout the storm-tossed time of youth. When everything else sinks into forgetfulness, it will still be remembered "what mother taught me"!

4. THE MORNING PRAYER: A GAIN

It is a little more difficult to give the morning prayer a fixed place in our life than the evening prayer, because in the morning we feel strengthened by sleep and are in a hurry to get to our work. But if we thus seem to think that we cannot find time to say a morning prayer, let us remember the old proverb: "In prayer is no delay," and if there are other reasons—petty things that have hindered us—then let us summon our will and say to ourselves: *I want to!* The morning prayer is henceforth to have a fixed place in my everyday life and in my home, and I think everything will go well: In prayer is no delay.

Just as the evening prayer because of the significance of time is particularly adapted as a *protection* against temptation, so the morning prayer for a corresponding reason is especially fit to prove a *gain* to us.

When we arise in the morning, the day is facing us, and it is of importance that we approach our work with willingness and high hopes—whether the work be that of the intellectual or the manual laborer. But, how often is it not the case that we approach our work slovenly and sourly—with the consequence that we feel it a burden and a difficulty. We do not discover that rest and that joy in the work which God bestowed upon it. The work becomes nothing but unwillingly done toil, and the day seems long and weary.

By way of suggesting a preventive I know of nothing better than to start the day with a morning prayer. It stimulates the willingness to work, to begin the day by thanking God for the night that has vanished, and to pray for blessing upon the work of the coming day. It imparts joy of living. It makes it easier to discover the rest and the delight in work, no matter how exerting that may be.

How often is it not the case that the man who is ready to go to his work, gets up silently and grouchingly, washes himself and sits down at the table: Breakfast is not yet ready, and his wife gets for this reason some nagging reproaches. At last the meal is served. Silently the man partakes of his breakfast, takes his hat and his dinnerpail, remarks sulkily that now he is going—and goes. Such a start promises a cheerless day for both man and wife. He goes to his shop or field with head bent low and his mind heavy while his wife takes up her duties at home—without cheer.

How different would not the *day* and the *work* be for the man and wife if they could unite in a little morning prayer and part with the words of the poet upon their lips:

Then gladly we go
Each to his work
Relying upon God's grace.
Thus gaining strength
To be of use, as God wills
In the very best way we know.
And that applies to all of us.

We all need to be told that we should go to our work with more gladness, rely more upon the grace of God, get more and more strength and joy wherewith to do our work so as to please God. To this end, the morning prayer is an incentive, and that is why I consider it a *gain*.

Just as the time of youth is the period when we stand most in need of the evening prayer because the temptations then are the strongest and meet with least resistance on our part, so we need the morning prayer the most at the time of maturity because it then is of particular importance that we

— — gain strength
To be of use, as God wills,
In the very best way we know.

This does not mean that there is any time in our lives that we do not need the evening prayer as well as the morning prayer. Indeed, we need both throughout our entire life, for we are always in want of protection against temptations, always in need of gaining increasing joy of living and happiness. Therefore, let us give both a fixed and permanent place in our everyday life and thus try to become "steadfast in prayer."

And in that steadfast prayer *the Apostles' Creed* and *the Lord's Prayer* must be absorbed as an inseparable part.

ZACCHÆUS

1. *TO BE HOME BY ONESELF*

"AND, behold, there was a man named Zacchæus, which was the chief among the publicans, and he was rich."

Consequently he must have been a happy man, many would think, for the conditions of happiness are riches and prominent positions. But Zacchæus was no happy man.

He may, of course, have experienced a certain degree of delight or happiness while he was so busily occupied in making money and in forging ahead until he reached the very top of the publicans' ladder; now, however, when he had accomplished all that—he was not happy, at all.

How could that be?

I believe at that time perhaps he *had lived his life outside himself, as it were, and been wholly absorbed by his official duties.* But now that he found time to be home by himself, and to be occupied with the inner world of his soul, he heard in there an accusing voice which told him: *You are a sinful man, Zacchæus!* And the man who is sinful, is not happy.

What should he do?

He might devote himself once more to the *mania for gathering wealth*, might thrust himself energetically back into the work. Or he might devote himself to the merry *life of society*—seek pleasures, the remedy which the world offers to those who are afflicted with wounded souls. But in both cases he would once more be forced to live his life outside himself. He did not like that. It would be too much like taking flight from oneself.

But there was a third way — *that of the repenting sinner*. He chose that. People referred to him by calling him a *sinful man*, and sighingly he had to admit that the people were right. He understood that now since he was home by himself — O, could but his sin be stricken out!

Now there was this Man, Jesus of Nazareth! Wasn't He the same one whom John the Baptist had spoken of as the Lamb of God, which taketh away the sin of the world? And was not He the same one who had said to a poor fellow sick of the palsy: "Son, be of good cheer; thy sins be forgiven thee!" If he might only see Him!

Suddenly streets resounded with the cry: Jesus of Nazareth is coming! Zacchæus got busy, ran on ahead and climbed unto a tree. Hidden by the dense leafage there, he would have a chance of seeing Jesus — why, He is coming right there — He actually stops at the tree, looks up, sees him, and says: "Zacchæus, make haste, and come down; for today I must abide by thy house!" And he made haste, and came down, and received Him joyfully. And when they saw it, they all murmured, saying that He was gone to be guest with a man that is a sinner. But Zacchæus stood, and said unto the Lord: Behold, Lord, the half of my goods I give to the poor, and if I have taken anything from any man by false accusation, I restore him fourfold. And Jesus said unto him: This day is salvation come to this house, forsomuch as he also is a son of Abraham. For the Son of Man is come to seek and to save that which was lost.

He was son of Abraham!

As Abraham had learned how to be home by himself and to say, "I am but dust and ashes" — thus Zacchæus had come home to himself when he realized that he was a sinner. And as Abraham was willing to sacrifice his son, his heart's treasure, thus Zacchæus had come to the point where he was willing to sacrifice half of what was his — that dear, dear property which his heart had loved so fervently and to which it had been attached for many years. That had been the most precious treasure of his heart.

To be home by oneself humbles. To live outside oneself makes haughty, and God is displeased with those who are haughty while He bestows His grace on those who are humble.

"For today I must abide by thy house," Jesus says.

Why? Because Zacchæus could be found at home. Jesus always knocks on the doors of those hearts where He knows He finds someone at home. He must abide there.

To the men of our own age the danger of living outside themselves in their work and business, is great. Our age suffers from a tension which was not known in bygone days. If a man is to surge ahead, he must let his business absorb his entire strength. Therefore, it is so difficult for Jesus to find men at home when He knocks at the door of their heart, and therefore so few men are to be found in the church on the Lord's day. Women are not in the same measure tempted to live their lives outside themselves.

But Zacchæus stands like one who admonishes the man of our age: *Try to be at home by yourself, in your own soul. That is the road you must wander if you are to find happiness.*

2. ALL FORGIVEN — NOTHING IN VAIN

"This day is salvation come to this house." To Zacchæus this means: *Your sin has been forgiven — all has been stricken out.*

Rev. Mr. Funcke relates how he on a certain occasion called upon Dr. Kögel in Berlin — a man who was paralyzed and unable to move. He pitied Dr. Kögel — regretted that this man, formerly so stately and erect, should sit thus crouching, but Dr. Kögel said: "Rejoice with me — God hath forgiven all my sins!"

In a cemetery in Southern Germany there are two tombstones with strange inscriptions; one reads: *Forgiven!* and the other, *In Vain!*

Beneath the former rests the dust of a woman who through her extraordinary beauty fascinated a number of admirers. They seduced her, made her run away from her husband and children, and when once she had entered the life of immorality, she went swiftly down the grade. She developed into a criminal and was imprisoned. In the penitentiary she came home by herself, and here Jesus found her. When she left the institution, she went back to her husband and children and proved a blessing to her home; as a humble, Christian woman she did not spare herself for the sake of those whom she loved. But when death drew near, she asked them to inscribe upon her tombstone that one word, Forgiven! This word was a world to her, was everything. Her sin forgiven by God, forgiven by mankind.

Yes, when *everything is forgiven* we can rejoice at being home by ourselves. But we need still one thing more before our joy is perfect. We want to be told *that we have not lived in vain.*

Zacchæus knows how to appreciate salvation. In proof of his gratitude he gives half of his goods to the poor. It is more blessed to give than to receive. Formerly he had felt a certain joy whenever he could add a sum of a hundred to his fortune — but how paltry that joy was compared to the joy of giving! That could not possibly have been done in vain.

Jesus said to His disciples: And whosoever shall give to drink unto one of these little ones a cup of cold water only, verily I say unto you, he shall in no wise lose his reward. No offering of thanks for salvation is in vain. It brings bliss. It will get its reward—from the greatest offer of thanks which we can afford to give, down to the smallest—a kind word, a friendly clasping of hands, a cup of cold water. Nothing of all this shall be in vain. But he who lives outside himself, absorbed by the cravings for ever more riches, lives in vain even though he may become a millionaire.

Are you not in need of having written above all of your life and all your doings that one great word, *Forgiven!* And are you not in need of being assured that you have not *lived in vain*? You may not have been able to bring the magnificent sacrifices which the world lauds in the newspaper columns, and you may easily be led into the belief that you have lived in vain; but then you shall know that the Lord who is the King of Kings and the Judge of all and everything, will reward also that which looks insignificant and small in the eyes of the world. Nothing of that which you do as His disciple, is done in vain.

Above the life of the children of the world one might place the inscription: *Nothing forgiven—everything in vain!* Above the lives of Christians: *Everything forgiven—nothing in vain.*

Isn't that so, then: Christians have glorious days!

WHAT TERMS DO YOU CHOOSE?

3. DURING THE FOLLOWING DAYS

It was a day of joy to Zacchæus when Jesus entered his house. But how were the following days?

Undoubtedly there were days when the old greediness tempted him again. When the people of Israel in a miraculous way had been helped across the Red Sea, they were saved from the armed hosts of the Egyptians, but not from their plagues. The Egyptian soldiers had been drowned in the waves of the Red Sea, but the Egyptian temptations accompanied Israel across the sea and made the wanderings in the desert beset with hardships and difficulties. Indeed, they often, in their worldly hearts, reverted to the thought: *Would it not, after all, have been better to return and to partake of the plentiful provisions of Egypt than to fight their way laboriously onward to the promised land?*

Likewise the tempter undoubtedly has often whispered to Zacchæus: After all, wouldn't it have been wiser to *gather money than to give it away* as an offering in return for salvation? But then Zacchæus in his mind reverted to that great day when Jesus for the first time was a guest in his house, and his thoughts have lived that day over and over again — No, never was I as happy as on the day when I gave half of my goods to the poor, and never have I been able to make as many people happy as on that day. The offering had not been given in vain. So the old greediness had to yield to the benevolent impulse.

But that very same thought may come to you and me: Wouldn't it, after all, be wiser to get a lot of money together than to give it away in the name of the Lord to mission work, to churches and schools, to the poor, the sick and the suffering?

No! And once again: No! For that person in whose heart greediness has triumphed, has lived in vain even though he may have gathered thousands of dollars. He has contributed to the increase of the *lifeless capital of mankind, but not to its joy of living, to its happiness.* But he or she who brings offerings in the name of Jesus, increases the joy of living and happiness of mankind by just that much. Perhaps he has struggled along laboriously to reach the promised land of joy and happiness. His life has attained a meaning both to himself and to others — and he has not lived in vain.

THE MARCH OF EVENTS

(Lu. 24, 29)

"ABIDE with us; for it is toward evening, and the day is far spent."

Thus the two disciples spoke to Jesus in the afternoon of Easter Sunday when they were at the village called Emmaus. The march of events on Good Friday had excited them greatly: Should really the powers of evil vanquish even Him of whom they had expected that He would redeem Israel? This thought was so utterly distressing. And what would happen to themselves? For also within their hearts evil had a firm hold, and they were not able to conquer it.

Thinking along these lines the two disciples walked toward Emmaus. It was as though the heart would be crushed under the weight of the events, but then Jesus came, and He told them that the march of events was not a series of sad and distressing *chances*. It behooved Christ to suffer and then to assume His glory. This was felt as a relief.

Was this, too, *planned* by the God of Israel?

They were not quite able to comprehend it. Neither did they know who was speaking to them; but when they were at Emmaus and He made as if to go on, they implored Him: "Abide with us; for it is toward evening, and the day is far spent!" It was such a comfort to listen to His words. In them was that healing power which crushed hearts needed—O, would He but tarry with them!

So He went inside with them, and when He broke the bread, their eyes were opened, and they saw it was Jesus Himself—that very same Jesus whom they had believed perished under the burden of the events of Good Friday.

Then they did rejoice.

Yes, Lord, abide with us; for it is toward evening, and the day is far spent!

Let us first of all think of our own *life-day*. None of us knows how nigh is the evening. We may be near the final hour, both you and I, even though our hair as yet has no silver tinge. And if we, with this possibility in view, review the march of events in our own lives, we see much which we would like to change—if we but could. How often have not the powers of evil been victorious in our lives, as they were on that Good Friday! That thought grips the heart wistfully. And a little way ahead: That dark power death—"the difficult death" as a modern writer has said. O, how intensely we wish that so many things could be thought over and lived over once more!

But when we thus review the march of events in our own life, we sigh: "Hearest thou also us, thou Son of Grace!" For the only one who can relieve our suffering is Jesus Christ; His abiding by us as the *Son of Grace* is the great surcease, for He comes from Heaven with grace enough with which to cover all our shortcomings, all our sins, and with healing for all those wounds which have been inflicted upon us in the course of the march of events. It is, indeed, a blessing to know that just what we are yearning for from the very depth of our soul is what He rejoices most in giving us. We shall not pray in vain.

But it was not only what we had thought and what we had done. There was so much in the march of events which was sad and incomprehensible. Was that an evil power which from without, by chance, disrupted our life? Was it a series of happenings without aim, without meaning? In that case we stand in need of listening to the words of Jesus: It behooves you to suffer this, and then to enter into My glory. The saddest events in our earthly life are like dark viaducts which lead us forward to glory. They, too, lead us to salvation. It is relieving when this becomes quite clear to us. We feel like the disciples when listening to the words of the Lord: There is comfort and healing in them. And then we can rejoice even though it is toward evening. We have no fear, we shudder not, at the thought that *the end of the day* is drawing nigh—for that draws us closer to the glory, and death will be the last dark passage through which we must wend our way.

But if we look round about us it seems to me that it is toward evening for *this world*. The end of the long day of the life of the world is drawing nigh, and by the words of the Lord we know that the march of events in the last days will not be cheerful for the Christians. The powers of evil shall arise against the Lord and His church, just as they did during that Easter week, and they will unite in one final outburst of desperate strength for the purpose of conquering. Then it will be seen decisively once more that the church is fighting principalities and powers, the masters of the world, and the spiritual hosts under the sky. The bow will be bent for this final struggle — and the world already now is singing a hymn of victory.

What shall we do?

We can change the march of events as little as could those early disciples. We may try a struggle as did Peter at Gethsemane — may perhaps even inflict a small wound on someone, but in our use of the sword there is no prospect of victory. We must have Him with us who on that Shrove Thursday spoke to the henchmen of wickedness with such might that they fell to the ground at the very sound of His words. Therefore, we are in need of praying, Abide with us, Lord, not only as the Son of Grace, but as the *Lord of Strength* — indeed, as the Lord of Strength we need Him when we survey the march of events in the world.

As little as at that time is He now powerless. But as it behooved Him to suffer these things and then enter into glory, so it also behooves His church during the last ages to bear those sufferings which the march of events carries in its wake, and then enter into glory; but, the Lord of Strength will shorten those last days (Mat. 24, 22). Here it is once more true that these events are not so many sad accidents and painful happenings of chance without aim or meaning. No, they, too, must be made to serve the reign of the Lord, and to help the church on its road to glory. *But only the Lord of Strength is able to make the events work together in unison, under all circumstances, for the purpose of our sanctification.* Only He can make dusk of the evening change into dawn for His church.

Therefore, we pray: "Abide with us; for it is toward evening, and the day is far spent." Yea, abidest thou with us as the *Son of Grace* and as *the Lord of Strength* during the march of events, and assurest thou us more and more that no one is able to tear us away from thy hand! Assurest us that even the very darkest, the most distressing events, whether they affect the individual or the church in general, are merely dark passages which, through thy strength and grace, shall lead us forward to peace and joy, to eternal life and everlasting blessedness. Then we shall rejoice during the march of events.

THE LITTLE WHILE

ITS SIGNIFICANCE TO THE LIFE OF CHRISTIANS

IT was during Easter week that Jesus spoke the word about the little while in which the disciples were not to see Him, and in which they would be brought to the very brink of despair while the world enjoyed itself in a fleeting exuberance of victory. The little while with its deep, its hopeless sorrow lasted for the disciples from Good Friday until Easter Sunday, and, forsooth, their weeping was heartrending, their plaints most gripping. Jesus had been taken away from them, and they did not understand that it behooved Him to suffer this and then to enter into glory; nor did they realize that they would themselves, in a little while, be mature, so as to win the world for the Lord who now had been nailed onto a cross.

Darkness enveloped the earth for three hours so the rays of the sun were unable to penetrate it; but still denser was the spiritual darkness which had gathered about the disciples: There was no glimpse of light, no hope! For He who, as they had hoped, was to have redeemed Israel, had breathed His last on the cross. The words of the Lord were literally fulfilled upon them; they wept and lamented. At this moment they were unable to cling to the promise of the Lord: "I will see you again, and your heart shall rejoice and your joy no man taketh from you."

But were we able at this moment to see the apostles before us and to ask them: What do you think of the brief hours of despair in your lives—and especially of that which was the most sorrowful of all? I am certain they would answer: It was, indeed, a most significant "little while," and all the brief moments of despair throughout life have been so valuable that we could not have done without them. But if this were so, as far as the apostles were concerned, then it must be the same for us, and with this in view we will ask:

What, then, is the meaning of the distressful "little whiles" to the life of Christians? Those dark and burdensome hours when the tears moisten our eyes; and darkness gathers about our souls; those hours which we would rather be without but which we can so ill afford to dispense with. I might answer quite briefly thus: *It is during those moments that we are moulded by the hands of the Father as the children of light!* I know for a certainty that it was during just such moments that I became a servant of the Lord wishing from out of the depth of my soul to find the way from the evil world of deceit and darkness homeward to the eternal abodes of light. Therefore I thank the Lord also for those dark hours which came into my life, and therefore I by no means praise that man or woman happy who has known no such moments, but I do think he or she who has struggled through them to peace and rejoicing is happy.

In order to understand fully the meaning of the sad moments in the life of mankind, we will recall a few of the great men of God.

David was named the man according to the heart of God. But was he made that when he reached the highest pinnacle of his power and glory and when he with regal strength ruled the subdued neighboring nations?

I hardly think so.

It was rather during those bitter hours when he, weeping and barefoot, was forced to flee before his own son, or when he with his heart writhing in anguish prayed: "Create in me a clean heart, O God, and renew a right spirit within me!" It was during such moments when he crouched in humiliation that he became disgusted with deceit and falsity, with the doings of darkness and the evil lust of the flesh. It was in such moments that he learned how to yearn from the depths of his heart for life itself: "Where thoughts are pure and deeds are unblemished."

When Peter had denied his Lord and Saviour thrice in the courtyard of the high priest and was standing without, bitter and heavy tears rolled down his cheeks; never in his life had Peter detested that denial as he did just then. How hideous it looked to him—to have denied Jesus! Undoubtedly he was thinking by himself: O, could I but find an opportunity of proclaiming Him once more—then I should do it with all the strength and sincerity of my heart.

Or Thomas! We know that after hearing the testimony of the resurrection of Jesus he said: "Except I shall see in His hands the print of the nails,0 and put my finger into the print of the nails, and thrust my hand into His side, I will not believe." Then, when he sees Jesus again and hears His gently reproachful, "Blessed are they that have not seen, and yet have believed"—how Thomas must have been disgusted with his infidelity, and how he must have reproached himself because he had invited the evil power of doubt and unbelief into his soul. That was to happen nevermore!

These heavy hours were changed into rejoicing for such men. And it is the testimony of all men and women who have been blessed by the special grace of God that such "little whiles" have meant much to the development of their lives by giving it *direction, depth and sincerity.*

But how about you? Have you had similar experiences?

Many of you probably will say: We know the hours of distress—we also know how deeply depressing they may be. Even though we may not have wept and lamented, like the first disciples, because of the scorn and ridicule by the world, we often have shed tears that betrayed the presence of a wounded heart. But we did not go farther in our understanding of the meaning of the sorrowful moments. We have felt their pressure, but we have lost sight of their blessedness; we have been unable to discover the gain which they mean to our lives.

Look to the depths of your own soul and then tell me: Do you not feel the hidden connection between the sin, as it had attained power in your soul, and the pressure of the brief, sorrow-laden moments?0 Have you not also in such moments felt a truer, a more sincere and deeper disgust with the evil character of sin, than otherwise? Did not that wish soar upward from the very bottom of your soul: Would I were relieved of all that is evil so that I might live with "all my thoughts pure, and all my deeds unblemished"?

But if you have felt this, then you already are somewhat conscious of the blessedness of the moments of distress, for that is what is asked of us first of all. Without disgust with the evil being of sin we cannot renounce the devil and all his works and all his ways.

But is that all to which the brief, sorrow-laden moments can guide and help us? No—the faith of the disciples was strengthened during the little while. It is true that their faith wavered in that while, and that it looked as though it would collapse, but *this was not the agony of death, but the pangs of birth.*

Hitherto they had been accustomed to seeing Jesus and then believing in Him. Now *that* faith was to be born which would cling to him through His word without seeing Him. During the little while it looked as though Jesus had suffered defeat and the world had conquered. But after the resurrection the disciples saw the meaning of it all: Jesus had taken death upon Himself not because He was vanquished but because the Father, in His unfathomable wisdom and His eternal love, had thus decided it for the purpose of salvation.

They knew now that no matter how discouraging the outlook might be, no matter how loudly the0 world might proclaim its victory—His word was to be depended upon. And firm in this faith they went out to conquer the world for Jesus Christ after having received the spirit from Above. Often it looked to them as it did on Good Friday, but instead of weeping and lamenting they sang hymns of praise to the Lord fully convinced that He was the strongest. Their faith had been strengthened so as to bear the resistance of the world, and rejoicing had taken up its everlasting abode in their hearts. *The little while had been the hour of birth of the faith which was to conquer all the world, and gain the eternal state of blessedness.*

Thus the little dark moments have a meaning in the lives of Christians, aside from filling us with detestation of the evil ways of sin. They must be hours of birth through which our faith shall emerge renewed and invigorated until it appears as that firm faith which wins the great victory over the world.

And if there is anything of which we stand in need, in addition to being filled with horror at the phantoms of deceit, the evil ways of darkness—it is the firm faith and the eternal joy of blessedness which give us strength to become more and more the children of God, immaculate before His face, and by which we can be easily recognized as children of light in a world darkened by sin.

The world still rejoices and still—after a struggle of almost two thousand years—thinks it shall conquer the church of the Lord. Now and then we are told that in another hundred years Christianity will be something entirely different, adjusted to the0 trend of thought—or that it will have lost all its strength. When we face this haughty scorn of the world, we need the firm belief that although the world thinks it will triumph, it will still collapse. For the Lord is Almighty: The great powerful world will never be able to remain longer, or to progress farther, than He permits.

Then there is the joy which no one can take away from us. It is the joy of blessedness in which all the sorrows of life vanish, just as the pangs of birth are lost in the exuberant joy of the thought that a new human being has been brought into the world. It is with the joy of blessedness as with maternal love: It is made through travail and suffering, and no one can take it away from us!

Ah, how it irritated and angered Jews and heathen when they were unable to deprive the ancient Christians of this joy even in the moment of death! When Stephen appeared before the council, and his face was like the face of an angel because the joy of Heaven reposed within his soul—they cut to the heart and they gnashed with their teeth, cast him out of the city, and stoned him. But his joy they could not take away from him: Would that this might abide among us in greater fullness, for it is that very joy which gives us the touch of gentleness, mildness and loveliness!

The Christian may say about the "little whiles" that are full of vexation, what Joseph said to his brethren: "God made everything right in order to do what He now hath done, and to preserve life." The "little whiles" may be heavy with trouble and sorrow, but it is an irremovable truth in the church of the Lord that He changes them into good purposes in order to preserve our lives.

It must have been difficult for the disciples to understand the Lord's word about the "little while"—and it is difficult for us amidst our adversity to absorb thoroughly the fact that God will turn our sorrow into joy—that, forsooth, sorrow itself is pregnant with joy, shall become joy, and that these "little whiles" are necessary to the development and the ripening of the Christian life. It was only when the disciples had lived through the little while and seen the Lord once more that they understood His words. So also with us. The dark "little whiles" in our life are to be read—like the Hebraic scriptures—backward. Only when we have lived through these dark moments and when joy has found anew the way to our hearts, are we beginning to realize their meaning.

They were hours of redemption and hours of birth. Through them we became disgusted with the evil ways of sin to such an extent that the Son of man found it possible to set us *actually free.* They were the hours of birth for the world-conquering faith and for the everlasting joy of blessedness.

We have seen the Lord again when the hours of sorrow had passed, and we have felt His presence among us.

God made everything right in order to preserve our life eternal.

THE MIRACLE IN OUR AGE

(Acts 26, 8)

THE miracle!

Well, who believes in it nowadays? If it had been five hundred years ago, it might have been different, but in our educated age—no, we know better now! Science has spoken with the assurance of an expert and said: No miracles happen! Everything adheres to certain stringent laws; our researches have proved this, and the miracle has never existed except in the brains of undeveloped ignorant individuals.

Nevertheless we maintain in the church of the Lord that the miracle is a fact—as concrete a reality as was—the French revolution. The miracle does not thrive on the recognition of science, nor does it collapse before the shots which science fires against it. But when we maintain this, some people pityingly shrug their shoulders or smile haughtily while they sneer: How backward you people are! You certainly are not well posted in regard to the development and the intelligence of the age.

Let us see if speech of this kind cannot be effectively met so that we as Christians may retain our faith and still be developed and intelligent people.

1. THE MIRACLE AND NATURE

If we ask infidel science how everything originated, it answers: *Through evolution!* The world has developed during millions of years. But if we ask further: Whence and from what? You yourselves claim that *nothing originates in nothing*, then this world must, according to your own postulates, have originated in something, for your own fundamental claim is that it cannot have risen out of nothingness.

To this the general answer is that perhaps there was a small beginning, a protoplasm from which all things grew. But if there has been such a protoplasm, it certainly is an unprecedented miracle. Never at any later time has anyone beheld such a protoplasm through which an entire world arose, and in that case *all existence is based upon a miracle.* This has only been assigned to as remote a time as possible, and even though one had not freed himself of the miracle, it was not irritatingly present as a constant probability in the evolution of the world. For, to admit that an Almighty God created everything from the very beginning is synonymous with admitting the fact of the miracle as a constant probability. It is impossible for us to conceive that the Almighty at the time of the Creation should have so exhausted His powers that He now faces His creations as one who is utterly powerless. If His omnipotence made all things, then He must still be able, through that very omnipotence, to interfere, to mend and to increase, because in His wisdom He0 realizes that it so serves the promotion of his eternal plans.

Yes, but the *miracle is contrary to nature*, it is said.

Let us see! When Jesus at the marriage at Cana in Galilee turned water into wine, a miracle happened, and many believed in Him.

Water into wine! Is that really contrary to nature? Is it not the very same thing that happens in nature every summer when the water of the soil is absorbed into the tender roots of the vine and passes through its branches, finally becoming wine in the grapes? The turning of water into wine is no change which rests upon violation of the laws of nature. In nature this happens in accordance with those plans which are the guiding laws of the powers of nature. At Cana in Galilee it happened in another way, but the same thing was accomplished: Water became wine! There is unity in the achievement. Is there not also an inner harmony between the powers working according to plans and laws in nature, and those which work untrammeled through the miracle? I think that we here are facing a unity in those powers—a relationship as intimate as between the Father and His only begotten Son who rests in His arms. And when we witness other miracles in which this unity becomes invisible to us, I certainly do not think it is because the unity is absent, but just because we are too shortsighted to perceive it. But then the miracle is, after all, not contrary to nature when looked at profoundly.

But the miracle is in conflict with the *immutable laws* of nature, it is said.

Let us mention an instance. I fetch a silver dollar and throw it up in the air. According to the law of gravity, which is one of the immutable laws of nature, it falls toward the ground, but by a firm resolve and by the strength in my arm I may catch it and hold it in the air.

What happens then? Is the law of nature violated, or is it rendered ineffective? By no means! But another unit of power appears which in this case is strong enough to hold the dollar in the air in spite of the fact that the law of nature acts upon it with its power in order to lead it earthwards. By my firm resolve and by the strength in my arm something else happens than if I had not interfered.

Yes, you say, such an insignificant thing as a coin anyone may keep in the air. It is different when we speak about the immense system of the universe. But—do you know whether or not the entire universe with its countless astral bodies weigh more in the hands of the Almighty than a silver dollar in mine? I do not believe it. Then, what you and I may do on a small scale, God Almighty may do on the larger scale without annihilating the laws of nature. They act as usual, each according to its own plan, but God Almighty may interfere and cause that something else will happen than would otherwise have happened, in spite of the fact that the laws of nature retain their entire power.

Finally it is said that miracle is contrary to *our experience.*

Let us imagine an old sailor a couple of hundred years ago. Through more than a generation he had steered his vessel sometimes aided by wind and currents, sometimes against them. If he were told that a ship might be steered straight against the wind and the currents without sails, without cruising, without oar strokes, he would have uttered a fierce sailors' oath that such a story was a lie—wild imagination! No, he knew by *experience* what was the power of the wind and the currents, and he had been struggling ever so gallantly against those very powers of the sea—no, no—don't tell me stories like that! You may be able to find some unexperienced people who will believe tales of that kind, but I know better.

Meanwhile we all know nowadays that the proud vessels sail steadily against wind and currents without canvas sails, without cruising manœuvres and without oar strokes. What is the reason for this? Are wind and currents adhering to other laws in our days, or has their effect been changed? No, not at all! But the old salt thought that his experience was exhaustive in this special field. It all required a power which he did not know, and in whose existence he did not believe.

The attitude of the unbelieving science in our age toward the miracle is exactly like this. It has emitted many a droll sailor's oath to affirm that the miracle is contrary to its experience—and with the very same justification as did the sailor. We all need being reminded that human experience is very, very limited. It embraces such a small fraction of the universe, and it is not inclined to concede1 its limitations. The handicap of science is that of the sailor. In order to steer his ship right against wind and currents a power was required which he did not know and in whose existence he would not believe. In order to let the miracle happen, a power is required of which science, as such, does not know and in whose existence it refuses to believe.

How many unbelieving physicians have not sworn as drastically as did the sailor, that they could not share the Christian faith in resurrection? The physician says like the sailor: I know better — don't tell me stories! I have seen too often how that pumping machinery in the human body which is called heart, comes to a stop, and when the heart ceases beating, the eye is extinguished, and the body approaches the process of dissolution. Don't tell me anything about the resurrection of the dead. It is contrary to my experience. — And yet, all that is required in order to make this possible, is a power which he does not know, and in whose existence he will not believe.

He who was powerful enough to turn dust into man from the beginning, certainly is powerful enough to revivify that dust.

The existence of this power is recognized, and has been experienced, in the church of the Lord. But, here we stop by asserting that *that miracle in nature means that God works in other ways than those determined by the plans and laws of nature*. It is the very same power of God that works through the miracle as through nature restrained by laws.

2. THE MIRACLE AND THE CHURCH OF THE LORD

If, then, we leave the sphere of nature for that of the church to seek an expression of the power which is working here, we find one formed by Paul the apostle: *The power of the resurrection of Jesus Christ.*

But as God's power in nature chiefly acts according to certain laws and plans, unheeding them only now and then — so does the power of His Son in the church. It acts regularly, determined by laws and order, and unrestrained only now and then. In this there is, in both cases, a very great blessedness to be found. We have been created to abide by conditions which are determined by well-defined plans and laws, and we would be seriously troubled by being the objects of merely arbitrary and unrestrained powers.

When Jesus made bread for the hungry multitude in the desert, it happened through the free interference of powers — not in accordance with accepted laws and plans. But now suppose that the farmer were to expect bread in this manner — that certainly would lead him into a painful state of doubt: He had not sown his seed in the spring, for he was sure a miracle would be wrought so that the crop would be ready by harvest time. Summer elapsed and he looked anxiously for the miracle which was to bring him the crop. According to the ways of human thinking it lasted too long before the miracle happened! What painful restlessness and uncertainty! No, there is greater surety and satisfaction in the order predicated upon laws, that seedtime and harvest1 shall not cease, and that whatsoever a man soweth, that shall he reap.

But as God thus has endowed nature with His power so as to make it adopt certain laws with the end in view that man's worldly existence shall be based thereon, so Christ has endowed His church with the power of resurrection which works through His institutions according to laws, and *upon this action, regulated and determined by laws, rests the existence of Christians.* By doing so He has not, however, exhausted Himself or confined Himself so as to make it impossible for Him to work through other methods, but we are restrained even as are those means through which the power of His resurrection comes to us.

It would be wrong on the part of the farmer to demand that bread should be made in any other way than that which God has designed for its production from the soil — and it would be just as wrong on the part of Christians to demand miracles. We must abide by the church *in which the power of the resurrection of Jesus Christ acts, regulated and law-restrained, at the baptismal font and communion, upon all those who will choose the right attitude toward them.*

But has not the miracle, this unrestrained action of the powers, disappeared from the church? Miracles do not happen nowadays as in the time of the apostles.

People are often heard to speak like this, and here we must first of all call attention to the fact that one period in the history of the church may be profuse in miracles while the other is devoid of them.1 It does not go according to our desires and thoughts, but according to what the Lord in His wisdom deems well for the fulfillment of His eternal thoughts. Furthermore, our age is not in a very receptive mood for the "miracle" — it might face *the strange things* gapingly instead of believingly accepting the "miracle" as a "miracle" and give God the glory therefor. Yet I am convinced that the unrestrained interference of powers has not ceased in our age, but it takes place only according to the counsel of the Lord, and where receptivity is present. Nowadays, this applies especially in heathen lands and in secret where the faithful pray and receive unseen by the eyes of the world.

But, in this connection, I would call attention to the following: The greatest miracle is not that some sick person may be restored to health, or freed of some bodily weakness, but that *I, the sinner that I am, may be resurrected in spirit, soul and body, in accordance with the eternal thoughts of glory of God.* This miracle is a thousand times greater than that which took place at the door of the temple when Peter said to him who was lame from his mother's womb: "Rise up and walk!" For this does not apply to a certain part of the body nor to certain bodily weaknesses, but to *the entire being with all its weaknesses.*

This is the greatest miracle of all, and it takes place until the very end of time within the church of the Lord.

Here we truly have reason for saying: Praise be to God that we are not expected to look for the unrestrained interference of the powers for the sake of the restitution of our entire being, but that we1 can adhere to the regulated, law-restrained acts of the powers, fully convinced that the good work which is thus begun shall be completed in this manner, in spite of the devil and in spite of death.

The power of the resurrection of Jesus Christ does not work here in the same way as in the case of the resurrection of Lazarus; for there it acted unrestrainedly and visibly, even to the unbelieving Jewish people. Here it works invisibly, but none the less tangibly, and a far greater goal is to be attained. I am not to be resurrected like Lazarus to once more live under conditions of sin, and to once more face death. I am to be resurrected from death and from the conditions of sin wholly prepared to be at home in the halls of Heaven. In order to achieve this I am not to look for *sensations* and *movements* in bluish dimness, but to adhere faithfully to the regulated, law-restrained acts of the powers within the church of the Lord.

It is in the faith in this action of the powers that we are, with Paul the apostle, to look forward to the resurrection of all things. I do not think that through the power of the resurrection of Jesus Christ all things are to be restored to the extent, as some have thought, that even the devil himself is to enter into the kingdom of God and become a leader of angels as he had been before; nor do I think that the godless and the infidels will be placed among the Godfearing and the faithful in the Kingdom of Heaven without repentance and faith. But I do believe for a certainty that all things are to be restored according to the eternal1 design of God in which the power of the resurrection of Jesus Christ is allowed to act. And for that we are yearning within the church.

But nature also yearns; that, too, is subject to corruption. That, too, shall be freed of the thraldom of corruption into the glorious freedom of the children of God. When the power of the resurrection of Jesus

Christ has penetrated nature, then it will appear as the new earth in which justice abideth. But just as man must pass through death, through perdition, humanly seen, so the ancient earth must pass through death and perdition, and the scripture testifies with equal firmness in the case of both, that man must die and the earth must perish.

Then the great miracle has happened that everywhere in the life of man and in nature where the power of the resurrection of Jesus Christ is working, the restoration of all things has taken place, and the rest has been completely segregated from us so that it no longer may tempt or ensnare us. All bonds have broken. The miracle has been accomplished in its entire extent in accordance with the counsel of the wisdom of God — that miracle which was begun when the only begotten Son of God was conceived by a woman — that miracle which, as far as you are concerned, took place when He was conceived within you at the sacred moment of baptism.

It is said about the miracle of Jesus at Cana that it was a *token*, and that may be said about all the miracles of the Lord. But, of what are they tokens?1 Of the fact that His power can conquer everywhere, *in nature, in the life of mankind, and in the spiritual world.*

Tokens of His mastery of nature were witnessed at the marriage at Cana where He turned water into wine; when He stilled the storm on Gennesaret lake; and when He filled the nets of the fishermen: In the life of mankind when blind became seeing; deaf became hearing; the lame walked and the dead arose: In the spiritual world when Jesus drove the evil spirits away from those who had become obsessed by them — indeed, even the prince of the evil spirits, the devil, was forced to yield defeated. All these are tokens that the power of Jesus Christ can do everything, can master anything from the deep of the sea to the highest arch of the sky, and that it is capable of attaining victory in the struggle with principalities and powers, with the spiritual hosts of evil beneath the sky.

But these tokens, furthermore, are *small beginnings of the restoration* and when they have been perfected, everywhere and all-inclusive, then that new Heaven and that new earth where justice dwelleth, has become a fact.

God is the God of order. Therefore we find plans, system and laws in nature as well as in the church. It has been given especially to our own age to realize this so that an expression like "the law of nature in the spiritual world" has been recognized. Science has perceived this regulated, law-restrained order of things in nature as keenly as never before, but, alas, it became dizzy thereat.1 Otherwise it would have exclaimed even as Paul did: O, world of wisdom and power! Who would have known how to plan thus? Who would have the strength to subdue and master the giant powers?

In the church of the Lord we respond: *God the Almighty Father, the creator of Heaven and earth!*

An atheist was lecturing at a village in England and ended by self-confidently inviting the audience to take part in a discussion.

Then an old woman, her back bent with the weariness of life and years, arose, saying:

"Sir, I have a question to ask you?"

"All right, my good woman," the atheist answered, "what is it then?"

"Ten years ago I was left a widow with eight unsupported children. I had nothing but a Bible, but by following its directions and by believing in God I have been enabled to support my dear ones and myself. I am now approaching the grave, but I am perfectly happy, for I am looking forward to an eternally blessed life with Jesus. *My faith has done this for me: What has your way of thinking done for you?*"

"Well, well, my good woman," the atheist said, "please, understand me right — I have no desire to disrupt your happiness, but — —"

"O, that wasn't the question at all," the old woman interrupted — "don't beat about the bush, but tell us: *What has your atheism done for you?*"

Once more the atheist tried to evade the question,1 but the audience applauded the old woman so vigorously that he felt it necessary to withdraw, defeated by a woman who, during a life of hardships, had experienced the power and the blessedness of Christianity.

The late Dr. Ahlfeld in Leipsic once said in his final address to a class of children about to be confirmed:

"Infidels will shake their heads at your faith. They will speak of their unbelief as progress. They will tell you that progress has been made in everything, and they will ask you why you then should abide by the ancient faith. Then you shall answer: The ancient sun has shone for thousands of years, and no one can give us one that is better. We make no progress by rejecting it but by learning how to make better use of its rays. Thus, also, with Christ. He shines through all ages as the Sun of mankind. He is the very same today and tomorrow and in all infinity, and it is not progress to reject Him. We must learn how to make increasingly better use of the rays of His grace. That, children, *is our progress*!"

AMERICA — YOU ARE THE HOPE OF THE WORLD TODAY — —!

May, 1919

John 8, 36: If, therefore, the Son shall make you free, ye shall be free indeed.

Acts 22, 28: But I was free born.

WHEN Paul had been imprisoned at Jerusalem the chief captain ordered that he is to be scourged in an effort to make him tell the truth. Paul then asks: "Is it lawful to scourge a man that is a Roman?" The chief captain asks whether he is a Roman, and Paul says that he is. The chief captain goes on to say: "With a great sum obtained I this freedom," but Paul answers: "I was free born." It is a question of the right of free men in ancient Rome.

Under the ancient Porcian law which was later restored by the Sempronic, no Roman citizen might be scourged, and anyone who violated the Roman civil laws, was liable to a punishment which involved the loss of property and life. Of this, we realize how deeply treasured civil liberty and rights were in ancient Rome. The right of free men might not be assailed.

It is about this right that the chief captain says: "With a great sum obtained I this freedom!" But Paul answers frankly and proudly: "I was free born!" *It is an heritage from my fathers.*

Thus the young generation in America may say: *We were born into civil liberty.* It is an heritage from the fathers. We have obtained it at no expense of our own. But the fathers of '76 bought it with their blood. When they fought under the command of George Washington, they endangered their very lives in order to win this liberty. Many sacrificed their lives. Indeed, it was dearly bought! When the Declaration of Independence was signed, Franklin exclaimed: "Now we all will have to hang together, otherwise we will hang separately."

But in 1860 the Star Spangled Banner waved above the heads of more slaves than there were inhabitants in the country at the time of the signing of the Declaration of Independence. So, for the second time America was plunged into a struggle for liberty for the purpose of making the Star Spangled Banner the true flag of the free. The spirit of '76 could not acquiesce in slavery. And through Abraham Lincoln it entered into a covenant with *the great, all-embracing and deeply sympathetic heart*—a heart so great that it could enfold the North and the South—so sympathetic that it was able to embrace white and colored people alike, friend as well as foe. This was the great heart that led America through the days of the Civil War—fortunately for this country.

It was this heart that beat in the breast of Lincoln when he as a 22-year old man down in New Orleans saw how human beings were sold in the same way as we nowadays sell cattle. Man and wife were sold to separate buyers and parted never to meet again—parted while they wept as though the heart should burst. Then young Lincoln raised his hand toward heaven vowing: "By the eternal God, if ever I get a chance to hit that thing, I will strike it and strike it hard." This was the Lincoln who led in the Civil War. The man with the great heart was equipped as no one else to win the victory, to *maintain the union of North and South and to gain freedom for the Negroes.* It was he who said, when victory was an accomplished fact, that he would continue the fight for the rights of man without hesitation, "with malice toward none, with charity to all."

But since the days of the Civil War America has gained a wealth which no other country has ever possessed. You young people are born to claim that, too.

Our youth was born to wealth and to inherit the forefathers of '76 as well as Lincoln, the man with the great heart.

It is, indeed, great to be born to all these things. But it is not easy. It requires a strong and alert youth to make the right use of such treasures.

Added to this it must be remembered that America after the Civil War was reckoned with as one of the Great Powers. When problems of world significance were to be settled, the question was asked: What does America say about it?

Came then the great world war. America stayed out as long as possible. The world began to reckon less with us than before. Germany even thought she could sneer at us with impunity.

How was that? Was it a matter of distance only? No, in Germany the belief prevailed *that the spirit of '76, and the heart of Lincoln's day had died within the bosom of young America.* At all events, it was not inclusive enough to span the great ocean and to sympathize with those who were suppressed and suffering yonder. It was with young America as with the wild animals caught and put into a cage: They are led into a life of ease and indolence; they lose their strength, their elasticity and their power of propagation. In brief: *Ease and indolence kill them!*

Similarly, it was thought *prosperity* had killed the spirit of '76 and the all-embracing heart of Lincoln in the youth of America, and under those circumstances there could be no danger that American youth would enter the great world war where prosperity and all kinds of comfort and ease were to be sacrificed and life itself be risked.

Miss Grace C. Bostwick writes in *The Pagan*:

O America!
They said you were young and crude and extravagant,
And that your women were too free and open;
That your children had no respect for age;
And that you gave no thought to the past.
They said you had no artistic sense
And accused you of setting up an altar
To the almighty Dollar — —
O America!
And they smiled when your name was mentioned.
But yesterday

There marched an army down the street,
An army of brave-eyed men with boyish mouths,
Straight-backed and proud in their new-found mission —
The saving of the world!
And yesterday . . . somewhere . . . at sea
A white face floated
With empty eyes upturned to an unseeing sky.
And yesterday . . . in a barren field . . . a mere boy
fell from his perilous work on high —
While great ships heavy with sustenance
Plow stolidly through the deep . . .
O America!
You are the Hope of the World today.

Germany had made a miscalculation; the spirit of '76 was not dead in young America, neither was the great heart of Lincoln. Prosperity had not been able to kill them. When the suppressed really needed America, our youth heeded the summons. With firm footsteps, with eyes afire, they went away into the great fight. I do not know whether they vowed as did the young Lincoln, but I do know that when they arrived at the battlefield, they struck, and struck hard — so hard, indeed, that the tyrant succumbed. And well may we say about that right of free men which was won by American participation: *It was dearly bought by you — who never came back.*

It is said that the French government in July, 1918, had decided to order the evacuation of Paris, but when General Pershing heard this, he telegraphed a request to postpone the carrying out of the order until his soldiers had entered into active fighting. Then came the turning point. Our soldiers brought it about, and victory was won.

But a new element has entered into the history of the war — into the relations among nations. It is the word of Jesus: "Therefore all things whatsoever ye would that men should do to you, do ye even so to them." Never before has this maxim been accepted as the *Golden Rule* governing international relations. President Wilson has repeated it time and again, and it characterized our participation in the war, even to the extent that our country has paid for the damages made to French soil when our soldiers dug their trenches. And this was but right. America did not enter the war with the intention of conquering or destroying one hair-breadth of ground. So we are justified in saying to Germany: You must pay for what you have destroyed, to the best of your ability.

"Whatsoever ye would that men should do to you, do ye even so to them!" By this we have arrived at something new. Our participation in the war constituted a great sacrifice of lives and money without any expectation of indemnity of any kind. But in this we find something of the redemption from the *thraldom of greediness* — something of that freedom to which Jesus will guide mankind. But that freedom is won only by the aid of the spirit of the Lord. And it seems to me that the spirit of '76 and the heart of Lincoln have entered into a covenant with, and have shown a willingness to be guided by, the spirit of the Lord.

Where the youth of America marches forward to fight in accordance with the spirit of '76 and with the great heart of Lincoln, guided by the spirit of the Lord, it is an unconquerable army and will always carry home the victory.

With Lincoln we can say: Victory is won, but the fight is to be continued without hesitation, with malice toward none, with charity to all.

I believe that America is destined to lead the nations of the world in the future, but if this is to succeed rightly, then our youth must make it clear to itself that it faces the choice between *the altar of the living God and the altar of the almighty Dollar. For which of these will you young people spend your strength? At which of these altars will you pray and praise?* The eyes of everyone look toward America as never before: "O, America! You are the Hope of the World today!" Is this truth to remain? It depends on you, young men and women — depends on your choice of altars.

Once upon a time there was a man who was permitted to wish whatever he wanted, and his wish would be granted. But he was to wish only once. Finally he made up his mind to wish that everything he touched would turn to gold. First he touched the door post. It turned to gold. He rubbed his hands delightedly: What a nice big piece of gold! It certainly was fine that his wish was as sensible as this! Then he started to wash himself, but the water turned to gold. That wasn't quite as delightful, but he let that pass. After that he sat down to eat, but the food turned to gold. He then realized that the fulfillment of his highest wish would lead him into certain death.

Likewise there are people in America who wish that everything they touch turn to gold. The result of everything they do is to be converted into gold: We name them profiteers. They kneel before the shrine of the almighty Dollar. But this means certain death to the spirit of '76 and to the deeply sympathetic heart of Lincoln, and the spirit of the Lord expires through this worship of gold. They think of themselves only. They are enslaved by the fetters of greediness. They refuse to do to others what they wish others should do to them. Are they to get the upper hand? It is for you, young people, to answer! The future of America lies in your hands. What is your choice?

Professor Georg Fr. Nicolai of the University of Berlin during the war gave expression to thoughts of such a nature that he was forced to flee from Germany to Denmark. It was there that he in October, 1918, wrote as follows:

"There are times in the history of mankind when we dare not put new wine into old bottles (Mar. 2, 22). We require new wine, new bottles, new thoughts and new men. In order to give the peoples of the earth faith, an inner awakening is required. The Bible speaks of it as repentance.... Less pathetically we moderns refer to it as the new adjustment. But no matter what name we bestow upon it, it stands to reason that without an awakening no new life can be produced....2 The process of dissolution is so far advanced that today the Biblical word has become true: Only he who giveth his life, shall keep it.... A new spirit must be inculcated in the peoples."

A new spirit must be inculcated in the peoples! That is the decisive factor for the happiness and the health of the nations in the future. Political spirit of liberty is not enough. Inspired by that you may fight and conquer and — set your foot upon the neck of the foe. No, a new spirit is needed. It is that spirit which, redeeming, speaks through the words of the Lord: "Whatsoever ye would that men should do to you, do ye even so to them!" That's the task that confronts you young people. It may not possess the tension and the excitement of the battlefield — it may not, perhaps, let you directly feel that you are taking part in the solution of the great problems of the world's history — it is, nevertheless, THE very greatest task of the world. Here we must be impelled by the spirit of God.

It is related about Samson how "the spirit of the Lord came mightily upon him." But while the beginning was good, the end was sad, for at last he was driven only by lust. Therefore he was of little blessing. He ended by representing mere brute force and no more.

I have seen the glow of the spirit in the eyes of the young when they went to war. In the beginning they were moved by the spirit of the Lord. Now the task is to continue in that spirit and thus continuously to remain "the Hope of the World" — not to end in materialism and as representing no more than brute force.

America is wealthy enough, strong enough, to attain a leading position in the ranks of the nations — to enjoy an age of greatness as did Germany. But in that case the collapse is sure. It is but a short distance ahead. We will have to face it — as Germany now has faced defeat.

Germany had been saturated with Darwinism. Looked at from one point of view, it is an emphasis placed upon brute force and upon the survival of the fittest. Added to this came the materialism which laid stress upon the values of what was materialistic and mechanical at the cost of the soul. The nation grew great and strong. But man became petty and insignificant. No nation has ever possessed such a wonderful and perfect mechanical development as that which Germany had reached when the war broke out. On the strength of that, the dominion of the world was to be won. But here, too, the words of the Lord apply: "For what is a man profited, if he shall gain the whole world, and lose his own soul?" (Mat. 16, 26). What profited it Germany that she possessed her soul-less mechanical attainments, even though they were ever so wonderful and marvelous? What would it have profited Germany to have gained the whole world when she would lose her soul thereby? No, then the great defeat certainly was to be preferred. Through that Germany may recover her lost soul. If ever any new adjustment was needed, it is there. A new spirit must be inculcated in the people.

But what would it profit America if she won the rank of a leader among nations through her strength and wealth? Nothing at all. The great collapse would be only a short distance ahead. Before or later we would succumb to it.

Still I believe that America possesses the qualifications for leadership as no other nation in history does—the leadership of that new adjustment which the world must needs experience if life shall ever again become sufferable upon this old earth of ours.

Why is it that America has superior qualifications? Has not England the very same qualifications? Are not the English the great commercial nation which embraces the earth with its countless ships? Or France—that liberty-loving nation with its technically wonderfully developed language? Now when everything settles down again, will not these nations be able to assume the leading position in the history of the world just as well as America?

No.—And I will attempt to explain why they cannot.

America has been created through a mingling of all the peoples of the world, as it were. It is true that some claim all the rogues and scoundrels of the Old World came over here—and some of them undoubtedly did. But it is not they who have built up America and made her great and strong. Nor is it those people of whom it requires twelve to make a dozen—for that species generally dies where it was born.

No, they who built America were men and women who possessed the great *daring* and that *strength of the will* which were necessary in order to carry them across great stretches of water and land, to make them fell the vast forests and break3 the prairie soil, and to build their homes in the woods and upon the prairies. These are the people who built America — who made the country great and strong and wealthy.

Many have feared that the daring and the strength of will of the fathers had died. The younger generation had too markedly become a *candy, kid-glove, silkstockinged youth*. But yonder on the great battlefield it found an opportunity to show that it still possessed the daring and the strength of will of the fathers. Once General Pershing had to retire his troops one mile. It was reported to headquarters, and the reply came back: "Push your men a little farther back and let them rest!" But by that time General Pershing already was preparing to storm forward again. And so unexpectedly swift and vigorous was the attack that not only was the lost mile regained, but one in addition. It was the daring of the American soldiers that won in this instance. And, speaking generally, it must have been the *daring* and the *strength of will* of the American soldier that conquered the *mechanism* of the German army.

The daring and the strength of will of the fathers still live on in the young generation: It is a contribution from all the peoples of the earth which no other individual nation can boast — and it is one of these very qualifications which make it possible for America to lead upon the great stage of history.

But, in this respect it is of still greater importance that America by receiving this contribution from all the peoples of the earth has developed a3 *deep-seated and sincere feeling of community* with all nations. Through the Irishmen here, America is in close contact with Ireland, through the Poles with Poland, through the Bohemians with Bohemia, through the Danes with Denmark, and so on. This adds to the qualifications which fit America for assuming the part of the leader in the progress of the world, and is in itself a qualification which no other country at any time has ever had, and which no other country most likely will ever have at any time in the future. There is no nation in the world which has such a *vivid and natural consciousness of community* with as many peoples as has America. And this is of unprecedented importance. For that nation which is to lead the world during the period of *readjustment* which the world so sorely needs, must do so, not through power and wealth, but through a deep-seated sympathy and a readiness and ability, born of that sympathy, to lead the many nations forward to something better—to a higher and nobler national life so that they will strive to live according to the words of the Lord: "Whatsoever ye would that men should do to you, do ye even so to them."

But America loses this unique qualification for leadership among the nations, on the day when the multitudinous languages spoken here die. Therefore, the great question is whether or not progress in this respect is to lead into that narrowmindedness which kills the many tongues. Or, will the development favor a retention of the native languages of the various nationalities here together with English? *English is the great common language of3 America—the principal language which must be learned by the immigrants.* This is so obviously a matter of fact that it really should be unnecessary to allude to it. But, in addition, every nationality should be allowed to retain its native language in order to ensure for America the preservation of that deep-seated natural sympathy with the many peoples created by God—"of one blood all nations of men." The American nation is related to all other nations. It therefore has the qualification for *understanding them* and *for encouraging the feeling of brotherhood* among them which no other nation ever has had, and which any other individual nation most likely never will have.

The history of the world is like one great and magnificent epic. Each nation constitutes a song in the poem. England has its own song—France has its own, and so forth. America has its own great hymn, but, in addition a large number of little songs, each has its own particular rhythm derived from the manifold living languages spoken here, and they add *richness* and *volume* to the mighty chorus.

Let me use another simile: We all know the Mississippi River. It runs from a point 'way up in the remote northwest, winds its way east and south until finally it releases its immense masses of water into the great sea. How does the river get these immense masses of water? The answer is that on its way it absorbs one little rivulet after another. Humming and rippling from cheerful little wells here and there they come, and every little rivulet, no matter how pitifully small and3 insignificant it may look, helps the Mississippi to become the great river which carries its tremendous volume of water to the sea.

Likewise, the American language is the great river which receives its cheerful additions from the many smaller living languages. Each springs from its own particular source, singing its own particular tune, and each language makes its own little contribution in order to make the American language powerful and great and to give it that wonderful volume which enables it to run into the great sea of the life of nations carrying with it a blessing of wealth like no other language. And the many individual peoples will, when they hear the English language spoken from America, feel that it comprises such a strange richness and volume as they are unable to find elsewhere. Indeed, it is almost as though they would hear the American people address them in their own respective language — that "wherein they were born" (Acts 2, 9).

Ah, you young generation! Behold this — and understand it! You are born not merely into the wealth of your land and to take up the heritage of your fathers. But you are destined for *a glorious future*, for a future achievement so great and magnificent that no young generation in any other country has ever seen the like.

You, young man, and you, young woman — you have been chosen to draw the strength and vitality of life from a multitude of small wells within your own field and to derive such sustenance from them that you can form your lives beautifully and harmoniously. And you have been chosen, in the spirit of brotherhood, to lead such a current of pure thoughts and elevated ideals to all the peoples of the earth in such a manner as to cause them to wonderingly ask: How is all this? We hear them speak the American tongue, and yet it is as though we hear them speak to us in our own language — in that "wherein we were born." It sounds just as home-like and peculiarly attractive as our own—because it has been enriched by many tongues. And the vital richness and fulness which it carries to them has gained from the fact that we here have had such a multitude of wells to draw from.

Therefore we, who are older, bend our knees and pray as did David (Ps. 144, 12): "That our sons may be as plants grown up in their youth: that our daughters may be as corner stones, polished after the similitude of a palace!"

What we want—is this: Strong erect young men, sons of America, who perceive, with the clearness of the spirit, the problems of the future and who, with the red blood of youth coursing in their veins and the glow of enthusiasm lingering in their eyes, will take up the task of solving them.

And, moreover: Pure and noble women: David had been looking at the corner stones that were to support that temple which was to be the tangible expression of Israel's ideal life, that of community with holy and just God: How beautiful they would be when they were polished—and how strong! Indeed, they were able to support that wonderful temple which was to be built to the glory of God. And then he has been thinking: O, Lord, give us women like these corner stones! Pure, noble, and3 strong women who can be the very foundation of the home-life of our country—and carry it into the community with God!

Paul the apostle writes in his epistle to the Philippians, 2, 5-11:

"Let this mind be in you, which was also in Christ Jesus: Who, being in the form of God, thought it not robbery to be equal with God, but made Himself of no reputation, and took upon Him the form of a servant, and was made in the likeness of men, and being found in fashion as a man, He humbled Himself, and became obedient unto death, even the death of the cross. Wherefore God hath highly exalted Him, and given Him a name which is above every name, that at the name of Jesus every knee should bow, of things in Heaven, and things in earth, and things under the earth; and that every tongue should confess that Jesus Christ is Lord, to the glory of God the Father."

Jesus Christ won the name which is above every name because He served mankind as no one else had done, and gave His life for its sake. Thereby He became the Saviour of men — their great leader who can guide them into eternal life and blessedness. Thereby He also became *the Lord* to the glory of God the Father.

During the war America gave herself to the service of mankind as did no other nation. Therefore the suppressed looked to America quietly imploring for aid, and therefore it might be said truthfully, especially in 1918: "O, America, you are the Hope of the World today!"

Now the question remains: Will America continue3 to be the great, unselfish servant among the nations, above all others, leading them into the riddance of the thraldom of greediness, guided by the spirit of the Lord? Then — if she does — she will win a name above the names of all other nations, because she will be the great servant who shows the way to the highest ideals — to the pure, charitable and peaceful thoughts among nations in that national and human brotherhood for which God created them: Of one blood all nations of men.

This I wish with all my heart. But it devolves upon you, young people, to answer. It devolves upon you to determine whether this will continue to be true:

"America! You are the Hope of the World today!"

God bless you, America! — God bless you with all your homes and with all your youth!